Praise for *Out of Circulation*

"*Out of Circulation*, the romantic suspense by Heather Day Gilbert, is a fun ride with clues and surprises along the way. It reminds me of Janet Evanovich's Stephanie Plum and Ranger."
~ **Jan Thompson**, author of the *Savannah Sweethearts* and *Seaside Chapel* series

"A spunky, quick-witted librarian who knows how to handle a firearm. An irresistibly imperfect alpha male hero who desperately wants to be a good man. Add a slowly unraveling mystery and Heather Day Gilbert's well-seasoned prose, and the result is a romantic story I'd check out again and again."
~ **Christina Coryell**, author of *The Girls of Wonder Lane* series

"Fans of romantic suspense and inspirational romance will fall in love with Ace and Katie as they race against time to satisfy the demands of a vicious crime lord. This faith-affirming, sweet romance novella is the perfect quick read for a rainy afternoon. Don't miss it!" ~ **Serena Chase**, USA Today's Happy Ever After blog, author of the *Eyes of E'veria* series

OUT OF CIRCULATION

Hemlock Creek Suspense Book 1

Heather Day Gilbert

Out of Circulation
By: Heather Day Gilbert

Copyright 2016 Heather Day Gilbert

ISBN-13: 978-1530811137
ISBN-10: 1530811139

Cover Design by Deranged Doctor Design

Published by WoodHaven Press

Series: Gilbert, Heather Day. Hemlock Creek Suspense; 1
Subject: Romantic Suspense Stories; Genre: Suspense Fiction

Author Information: http://www.heatherdaygilbert.com
Author Newsletter: http://eepurl.com/Q6w6X

Other Books by Heather Day Gilbert:

Miranda Warning, Book One in *A Murder in the Mountains Series*

Trial by Twelve, Book Two in *A Murder in the Mountains Series*

God's Daughter, Book One in the *Vikings of the New World Saga*

Indie Publishing Handbook: Four Key Elements for the Self-Publisher

1

Rearranging the new books, librarian Katie McClure reflected on just how completely her dreams had run aground.

Growing up, she'd always planned on joining the FBI, where her father had worked for fifteen years. But a permanent foot injury and her dad's early death had negated that plan.

So much for doing anything memorable or spectacular. It seemed God had a funny sense of humor, derailing her noble aspirations and sticking her in the podunk West Virginia town she grew up in.

"Miss Katie, where's the latest Georgia Ray book? I've read five in the series and can't find the next one."

Katie snapped out of her funk, directing the young patron to the correct Juvenile Fiction shelf. The girl's mother, searching for her own reads in Adult Fiction, shot her a grateful smile.

Returning to the New Releases shelf, Katie caught sight of a tall man she'd never seen at the Hemlock Creek Library before. He seemed out of place in his urban button-down and slim dress pants. His wavy, nearly-black hair set off crystal-clear blue eyes. He winked in response to her gawking, and she mentally kicked herself. Seriously. Her life was so boring that instead of bird-watching or stargazing, she'd resorted to nearly salivating over some handsome man perusing library shelves?

Sighing, she decided to reorganize the week's display books by color, starting with red. She'd worked up a small grouping of her favorite reads when she glanced toward the Reference section. Something caught her eye.

A man in a mask.

She didn't hesitate to scream. "Everyone hit the floor!" Why wait around to see if the man had a gun?

Her boss, Reba, shot her a quizzical look from the floor behind the front desk. Katie pointed toward Reference, breathing slowly and pondering what she could use as a makeshift weapon, should the masked man move her way.

Sure enough, black combat boots marched straight toward her. Probably hadn't been the smartest move to shout and draw attention to herself, but she had to do something to protect the library patrons—especially the children.

She slid a chunky, oversized book from the shelf, hoping to hurl it at the fast-approaching man. She was utterly exposed in the middle of the floor.

Out of nowhere, the dark-haired stranger crept her way, positioning himself in front of her. "It's going to be okay," he whispered.

As the masked man rounded the corner, his unnaturally golden eyes narrowed, taking in Katie's would-be protector before fixing on her. A shorter masked man with a submachine gun trailed behind him, glancing around nervously.

A thick, foreign voice filled the air. "Ms. McClure—"

How did he know her name? Had he targeted her?

She closed her eyes, breathing a prayer she couldn't even put into words. Seemingly in direct response, police sirens wailed and tires screeched to a halt on Main Street.

The men exchanged glances, then bolted for the side door that gave way to an outdoor reading area.

Everyone stayed frozen for a few moments. A slight whimpering sounded from the Children's Section, followed by a mother's soothing murmurs.

Katie's tried to de-escalate her ragged breathing. The man had known her name. But why? What had he wanted from her?

As police officers burst through the doors, the dark-haired man lightly tapped her shoulder, pulling her back to reality. He stood, thrusting out his hand to help her to her feet.

"Thank you." She tried to keep her balance, but stumbled into him, accidentally reaching for his waist to right herself. Her eyes widened as she realized he had a concealed gun tucked under his shirt. Guns weren't allowed in the library, but then again, it comforted her to know that if there'd been a shootout, he would have been armed. Who was this guy?

"So sorry." Her face reddened, and in return, the man dazzled her with a brilliant smile. For the thousandth time, she wished she could be more like her older sister. Molly didn't have a stumbling gait like her own. Molly's hair was a glossy auburn, while hers was a bright, flaming red. Molly always knew exactly what to say to men. Molly had boyfriends in droves, but refused to marry anyone with a salary under $120,000.

After an intense but brief conversation with the police officer in charge, Reba made an announcement on the library speakers. "The intruders are gone. Please gather in an orderly fashion in the conference room so the police can take statements."

"Ace Calhoun," the man intoned, drawing Katie's attention back to him. His voice was deep and had a decidedly Northern clip to it. "Nice to meet you. Good thing I was passing through today. I thought I'd get a taste of small-town life, but I'm guessing what happened here isn't a daily occurrence?"

She shook her head, still in disbelief. "Not at all." She took his proffered hand, giving it a weak shake. "Katie McClure. Thanks so much for trying to protect me." She kept her eyes on his chiseled face, but couldn't stop thinking about his concealed gun.

He seemed to read her mind. "Don't mention it. I'm just visiting from Manhattan. I came down to attend the Executive Protection Conference. I'm a bodyguard." He subtly patted his belt holster.

She nodded mutely, unsure how to respond.

A young police officer walked over to take their statements. It was more than possible that Ace didn't want the cops to know he was packing heat in the library, so she left out that tidbit as she explained the course of events.

When their statements were complete and the officer strode

off to speak with other witnesses, Ace smiled. "I really need to get going, but nice to meet you, Katie McClure. Here's my card."

He pressed a business card into her hand, but she pocketed it and watched as he walked toward the library doors. Pushing through the turnstile, he ambled out onto the street without looking back to notice her final wave. She doubted she'd ever see him again—maybe he was her guardian angel.

Ace Calhoun was on a mission—a mission he hadn't wanted to accept. But his boss wouldn't take no for an answer. "You have to do this job. You owe me one favor, then you're off the hook."

Pretending to be a bodyguard wouldn't be hard. He knew his way around weapons and bulletproof vests. And his orders—to charm a couple pretty sisters and gain access to their home—couldn't be easier.

But he hadn't expected company.

Those masked thugs had made it clear they were looking for Katie. Who had tipped them off? This would throw a massive kink into his plans.

In his calculated fashion, he'd already begun laying the groundwork. He had chatted up the oldest sister, Molly, at The Greenbrier Resort where she worked. Not only did she look like a model, she had been extremely receptive to his overtures.

And today he'd tracked down Katie McClure at the Hemlock Creek Library. She was taller than he expected— maybe 5'11. She had long red hair, just as described. What his boss hadn't mentioned was her liberally freckled skin, her button nose, and her grape-green eyes that peeked out from under straight red bangs and followed his every move.

In fact, she was a little more than he bargained for, with her hawk-like observational skills. Although she projected an innocent vibe, she had to be equal parts savvy, given how quickly she had raised the alarm for the masked men. And she hadn't mentioned his concealed Sig to that cop, even though she was aware of it.

One thing was certain: Katie McClure, wobbly as she was on her legs, was no pushover.

⁂

In a tradition they had maintained since Dad's death, Katie, her mom, and Molly gathered for a family dinner. Katie's brother, Brandon, had moved to Arizona before Dad died, while she was only in high school.

While Katie had always admired her dad's dedication to the FBI, Brandon had loathed it and resented Dad for all the hours he'd spent at work. The McClure women knew he had never forgiven his father, but they didn't know how to broach the topic when he visited every Christmas.

Katie was working on a salad when Molly burst through the front door, making her expected late entrance. Katie suspected her sister's alleged "overtime" consisted of chatting up wealthy old men.

Dropping her oversized purse and elegant trench haphazardly on the couch, Molly balanced precariously first on one leg, then the other, removing her strappy gold heels. Then she unbuttoned her blouse, stripping down to a fitted Pima tank top. Finally, she padded into the kitchen, her red toenails sparkling with each step. Molly McClure knew how to make an entrance.

Katie glanced down at her own clothing ensemble—Dad's oversized oxford shirt and her favorite beat-up jeans. Well, it had been a long day.

"Katie!" Molly dropped kisses on her sister's cheeks in an affected European fashion. "Mom told me what happened! Heavens to Betsy, are you all right?"

Katie nodded. No use going into details with Molly the Melodramatic, who would make the entire event seem like some kind of personal attack.

But wasn't it? They had known her name.

Lost in thought, Katie carried the salad to the table, while Molly busied herself cutting garlic bread. When the oven timer buzzed, Mom rushed in, gave Molly a peck, and set her bubbling veggie lasagna in the center of the table.

After they settled into their seats, Mom said the blessing and Molly launched into colorful descriptions of guests at The Greenbrier. Katie finally tuned in when she heard the words "New York City."

"...And this suave, smiling man from New York City came right up to the desk and produced this platinum card. Jessica flirted with him relentlessly, but I'm telling you, those Yankee men have that air of...*je ne sais quoi*. Longish black hair, arctic blue eyes, big muscles...dreamy."

Molly had to be talking about the mysterious Ace Calhoun she had met at the library—able to impress the female staff at The Greenbrier with a single smile. Being a bodyguard must be a lucrative profession, if he was able to afford such a high-class resort.

Molly shot her a look. "I'm telling you, sis, he was perfect. Come to think of it, he's your type."

Her type? Since when did burly Yankee bodyguards constitute her type? Molly was only looking on the outward appearance, which—granted—was very pleasing. Katie wondered what Mr. Ace Calhoun's heart looked like, which was the only thing that mattered. Still, she had to concede she'd been impressed with his noble attempt to keep her out of harm's way.

"I've met him," she said shortly.

Molly's gold-flecked eyes widened. "You're kidding me! How?"

Katie calmly forked up a bite of Ranch-drenched salad and took her time chewing it. This was too fun, keeping Molly in suspense. Instead of playing her usual role as homebody sister, she was now a woman of the world. In the know.

"We met at the library."

"At the *library?*"

Katie tried to ignore Molly's tone, which was loaded with sarcasm. "Yes. Occasionally people do come and go from the library, and sometimes—though rarely—those people are from out-of-state. Just passing through."

Molly looked like she wanted to jump out of her seat. "Yes,

but you said you'd *met*. You must have talked to him. What did he say?"

Not much, come to think of it. But she'd never admit that.

"Actually, he tried to protect me from those thugs. He got between me and their guns. Then afterward, he told me he was a bodyguard from Manhattan, attending a conference. I didn't realize it was at The Greenbrier. Pretty swanky conference, if you ask me."

Molly rolled her eyes. "Of course it is. I'm sure he's a top-tier bodyguard."

Katie snickered. Her sister was just making up that *top-tier* terminology, something she tended to do.

Molly's eyes flashed. "What are you laughing about? I suppose you're feeling special that he talked to you. He talked to me too, you know."

That much was inevitable. Most men fell over themselves to get Molly's attention. It was the way it had always been, even more so once guys noticed Katie's limp. She was not the popular sister.

Mom intervened. "Girls, girls. Have either of you talked with Brandon lately?"

Molly poured herself a refill of sweet tea. "I called him last night. He said he's been flying the helicopter more than guiding whitewater tours this month. I guess they have a new guy trained on the rafts."

"I wish he'd just come home. It's not like we don't have whitewater in West Virginia." Katie stabbed a piece of lasagna, sending veggies and noodles sliding on her plate.

Mom placed a hand on Katie's. "I know you miss him. When it's time, I believe God will bring him home to us."

Molly nodded. "You should call him sometime, sis. He asks about you a lot."

Katie knew she should. Besides, for once she had something interesting to talk about.

After cleaning up, they cozied onto the couch to watch their customary episode of *Gilmore Girls*, but Katie found herself yawning repeatedly. Even Lorelai's clever one-liners weren't making her laugh tonight. She finally stopped fighting the urge to conk out and stood up.

"I need to hit the sack. Reba wanted me to come in a little early tomorrow, just to regroup. I'm wiped out."

Molly frowned. She stretched her legs before grabbing for Katie's discarded blanket. "I don't know why the library isn't a crime scene or something. Why do you have to go to work after what you went through? You should take a sick day."

The idea was tempting, but Katie was no longer the kind of girl who took sick days. She'd been confined to bed far too long in high school after her foot injury. It made her value each day she could be up and around.

After giving Mom and Molly a hug, she walked outside toward the back door of her garage apartment, following the solar lights along the connecting pathway. The automatic light came on, illuminating glints on the ground that made her look twice.

Glass had been carefully swept under a bush and her porch broom was askew. As her gaze trailed up, it became obvious a glass panel on her door had deliberately been broken. What if someone lurked inside, waiting for her?

Gathering her wits, she walked as quickly as she could back to the house. She went straight to Dad's office, opened a drawer, and loaded the nine millimeter Sig he'd always carried. Mom's eyes widened as Katie emerged, holding the gun by her side.

"Wha—?"

"Call the cops. Somebody might be out there."

Molly gasped and slid onto the floor, cowering on the carpet. "Don't you *dare* go out that door."

Katie wasn't that stupid. "I'm not. I'm sitting here with the gun to protect your sorry hide."

Molly's slow grin assured her she wouldn't go into hysterics. You never knew what kind of drama Molly would bring to a situation.

"Thanks, John Wayne."

It took the police nearly ten minutes to arrive. When Katie saw them pull up, she unloaded the Sig and replaced it in the case.

She met them at the door and led the older police officer to her apartment. He motioned to the other officer, turning on his flashlight. Guns at the ready, they proceeded to comb over the three rooms. After what seemed like thirty minutes, they finally turned on the light and gave the all-clear.

She hesitantly walked in. It quickly became apparent what had occurred.

Everything had been turned over or ripped apart. Drawers

were emptied, their contents strewn about.

Katie righted her favorite wicker chair. What was this all about? Was this the work of the same gunmen from the library? What were they after?

The police asked her those very questions, but she had no answers to offer. By the time she trudged back to her old bedroom in Mom's house, she could barely hold her eyes open. There was no way she'd sleep in her apartment tonight.

Mom hugged her, mentioning that Molly had finally returned to her own townhouse in Lewisburg so she could work in the morning. They both knew the real reason was that Molly would be scared out of her mind to stay here tonight.

Reloading the Sig and placing it under her pillow, Katie dropped fully-clothed into her white canopy bed. What little sleep she had was riddled with nightmares.

2

Ace munched on a flaky, buttery croissant and washed it down with pitch-black espresso. He planned to visit the McClures' home later this morning.

Today he sported his turquoise polo shirt that always garnered female compliments, as well as several generous sprays of a newly-released cologne called *Hedonist*. A fragrance counter saleswoman had offered him the used sample bottle after he had sweet-talked her a bit. He hoped Katie McClure was so easy to tempt.

He had decided to focus on Katie. She seemed more level-headed than her sister. Chances were, Katie would be privy to any secrets the McClures hid. Anyway, he couldn't very well pump *both* sisters for information under the guise of dating.

Thinking of Katie's green eyes and serious demeanor, he found himself wishing he could make her laugh. If he could, maybe he could get close enough to accomplish what he was here for.

This whole job was utterly distasteful. What would his

granny have thought? Granny was the one person who had believed he could make something good of himself. She took him to church and told him God made him for a special purpose. He used to believe that, until someone framed him and he wound up thrown into the slammer. When God let him go to prison, he'd decided it was better to trust in himself, not in some God he barely knew.

Luxuriating in the shiny charcoal Lexus he'd rented with his boss' money, he couldn't deny that crime did seem to pay. Leather seats, sunroof…this was living the life.

He shook his head, focusing on the task at hand. Today he would take the next step in winning Katie McClure over.

◦≈≈◦◦◦≈≈◦

Breakfast was tense, the break-in still fresh in their minds. Mom had made Katie's favorite—French toast—but they both took only a few bites. As Katie sipped her strong coffee, the doorbell rang.

"I'll get it." She figured it was the police with more questions, and she had nowhere to go. Reba had decided to close the library today.

Mom nodded and Katie slowly made her way to the door. Her foot was always stiffer early in the morning.

Opening the door just a crack, she was dumbfounded to find Ace Calhoun standing on their front porch.

She forgot her manners. "What are you doing here?"

Ace smiled, and the effect wasn't lost on Katie. She had to admit he looked just as natural in jeans and a T-shirt as he did

14

in his trendy outfit from yesterday. He actually looked like one of the local "good ol' boys".

"I wanted to check in with you before I left. Your sister gave me your address."

She shook her head, tightening her lips. Of course Molly had been handing out her home address willy-nilly to good-looking guys. "Thanks. I'm home today because they closed the library."

"That's probably wise. I'm hoping the police have a lead on those guys?"

"Not yet." She didn't want to mention the break-in last night, since it was none of his business. "Are you flying out of Lewisburg?"

"Yes…in one of those tin-cans I flew here in, no doubt. But I need to get back to Manhattan. Bodyguarding waits for no one." He laughed.

Mom walked up behind Katie and put her hands on her shoulders. "Excuse me, but did I hear you say you're a bodyguard?"

Oh, no. Surely Mom wouldn't…

Ace nodded earnestly and produced an I.D. that read Kern Personal Security. Mom flipped it over, pulled it out to examine the back, and seemed satisfied.

"And you two know each other…how?"

Katie sighed. This friendly chatter could mean only one thing. Mom was going to invite Ace in.

"He's the guy from the library. The one who tried to protect me. He's flying out today—"

Mom placed a hand on her heart and interrupted her. "You don't say! Well, you just come right on in here and have some French toast, young man. It's the least I can offer for your bravery."

"I just ate, but I'd be happy to have a bite or two. Thank you."

Katie refilled their coffee and Mom heated the French toast for Ace. When she set the plate down, he scanned the table.

"What do you need?" Mom asked.

"Maple syrup?"

Katie pointed to the bottle of Mrs. Butterworth's. "Don't you see that?"

He hesitated, then reached for the bottle. "Oh, sure. I'm just used to real maple syrup."

She snickered, but Mom shot her a look.

"So, you're a bodyguard in New York," Mom probed. "I guess you've run into plenty of scoundrels."

Ace nearly choked on his bite. He took a big swig of milk. "Yes, more than I ever wanted to."

Her stomach sank. She knew exactly what was coming next.

"Ace, I tell you what," Mom continued. "We have a little problem here and I don't know what to do. Katie's apartment next door was ransacked last night. The police are looking into it, but I know we'd feel a whole lot better with an armed guard around. Now, I can't offer you much money, but I have some left in our retirement nest egg and I'm sure the whole family will go in on this."

Surely he'd say no. Manhattan would pay a lot better than

small-town folks ever could. She held her breath.

Ace glanced at her, then back at Mom. His gaze intensified. "I hate to hear that. And while I do have other work pending, I can have them call someone else in." He extended a hand. "Ace Calhoun, at your service."

She couldn't believe this city-slicker was willing to hang around Hemlock Creek. Yes, he knew how to carry a gun, but did he know how to deal with heavily-armed thugs like those library invaders? Something in his suave smile threw her off-guard, and she couldn't quite bring herself to trust Mr. Ace Calhoun.

Ace couldn't believe how easily he'd tricked Mrs. McClure. Yes, she had excused herself to call Kern Security for verification, but his boss had made sure his story checked out.

Katie was a different story. Those green eyes tucked under a fringe of red lashes were definitely more piercing than trusting today. As she stalked out of the kitchen, he noticed her limp was more pronounced than it was yesterday.

Ace followed her, easily overtaking her stride. "Did you injure yourself somehow?" He motioned to her foot.

The glare became more more serious, hostile even. "No. I have a permanent limp."

She said it almost like a dare.

Before he could respond, the front door opened and Molly whisked in. "Hey Katie, how's—" She nearly dropped the purse dangling at her elbow when she caught sight of Ace.

"Well, hello." She grabbed his hand, her smile brightening. "Nice to see you around."

"Thank you. I'm going to be in town a while longer. Your Mom actually hired me to protect your home until the police catch these guys."

"Oh, mercy." Molly fanned herself and winked at Katie. "Maybe I need to move back in."

He caught a barely-perceptible flash in Katie's eyes. Did she feel possessive of him? That was a good thing. But her words fell flat.

"He won't be staying here, I imagine. Maybe down at the Kingsbury Hotel."

"Is that the one I saw near the gas station? I'd be happy to move over there." Anything to stay close.

"With that Lexus and your…Manhattan job, I would think you could afford The Greenbrier a few more days," Katie mumbled.

"Katie!" Molly looked appalled. She shot Ace an apologetic look. "She's a librarian, you know. They spend too much time buried in books and not enough time practicing *politeness*."

Katie shrugged, walking up the hallway. Molly wasted no time, her warm eyes focused on Ace's.

"So. How do you like West Virginia? You know, I've heard West Virginia girls are the prettiest in the United States." She smiled widely.

He stayed noncommittal, ignoring her brazen overtures, even though her looks were definitely hard to ignore. "I'm sure that's true."

Katie returned, awkwardly balancing a bucket, broom, and cleaning supplies.

He grabbed the wobbling bucket before she could protest. "Where are we going?"

She glared. "*You're* not going anywhere. I'm going over to clean up my apartment."

Molly gasped. "You're not moving back out there, are you, with some home invader running loose?"

"I don't know. But I'm not leaving my things flung around like that."

"Let me help," he said. "It's the least I can do, and if those men come back…"

Conflicting emotions played on Katie's face. She finally gave in. "Okay, I could probably use an extra set of hands. Cleanup isn't Molly's thing."

Molly stuck her tongue out at Katie, but didn't deny what she'd said. "I'm going to find Mom. Let us know if you need anything. Especially if *you* need anything, Ace." She winked.

Ace trailed behind Katie, secretly pleased he'd gained access to her apartment. Maybe he could do some unobtrusive snooping.

Now if only Katie would respond to him as warmly as her sister. He determined to crank up his friendliness factor…or would that even work?

Watching Ace throw himself into cleanup duties, Katie felt somewhat repentant for her distrustful attitude. The man truly did seem committed to helping, and for the love of everything, he was *so* easy on the eyes. She pretended not to notice, but the way his muscles strained at his T-shirt sleeves attested to why he was a bodyguard. Not to mention he was packing a handgun that looked bigger than her dad's. Even though she hadn't gone shooting much since her dad's death, part of her was still impressed with a man who could handle a gun.

He caught her gaze. "It's a .45. That's a large-caliber—"

"I know what it is," she snapped.

"Sorry, I just assumed you didn't shoot. Most women I've met don't."

"Well, you aren't in Manhattan anymore." She didn't know what had possessed her tongue. She had never been this snippy in her life. She tried to soften her response. "I don't shoot these days. But I used to."

He nodded. She appreciated that he kept silent and didn't push the issue.

"So, tell me about your family, now that you've met mine," she said.

He unearthed a pair of her low heels, depositing them on the couch as carefully as if he were returning eggs to an upturned nest. "Not much to tell. I was closest to my granny, and she died when I was a teen. My dad was always busy at work…my mom wasn't really invested in my upbringing, I guess you'd say. I don't have any siblings."

She nodded. "And how did you come to be a bodyguard?"

He shrugged. "I watched my dad. He owned a gun store. He didn't teach me about weapons, but I watched him show them to others." Those intense blue eyes rested on hers. For one moment, Katie glimpsed the rejected little boy in the grown man.

Bustling around to soften his painful candor, she shoved all her clothes into a big trash bag to sort later. No need for him to go through those. As the weight of the bag increased, she found herself stumbling while she dragged it along.

He moved to her side, so quickly she didn't have time to react. He spoke softly near her hair. "I can get that for you."

Ignoring his understated woodsy scent, she pulled the stuffed garbage bag up with both hands, nearly toppling herself. "It's no trouble."

He gave her a slightly crooked smile, obviously amused. "Of course it's not." He plopped down on the couch, watching her.

"What are you doing? You could...put all the big spoons back in my drawer in the kitchen or something."

"Doesn't seem like you need my help." He stretched his arm along the couch.

"Of course I do! Why did you come over here in the first place?" The bag seemed to grow heavier as she stood.

He leaned forward, intense. "Then say it."

"Say what?" Exhausted with her façade of strength, Katie finally dropped the bag.

"Say you need my help. It kills you, doesn't it?"

She gasped. Who was this man, to come into *her* apartment and try to figure her out? To be so glib about her weakness? She would never ask him for help.

"Just because you're our bodyguard doesn't mean you're

allowed to mouth off like that. I can get this place cleaned up just fine on my own, which was my original plan." She started to whirl around, but her slower foot caught in a quilt on the floor and she tumbled onto the couch—uncomfortably close to Ace.

She expected him to take advantage of the situation, but instead, he stood and offered his hand, like a gentleman. She swallowed her pride and took it, allowing him to help her to her feet.

As they continued to work in silence, she kicked herself for her outburst. She had not been herself since this New Yorker invaded her hometown. Or rather, since those thugs invaded the library.

The urgent, nonstop barking of the dogs next door broke into her thoughts. Without thinking, she rushed out the door to see what the unusual ruckus was about. She could feel Ace hot on her heels.

Wheeling around the side of the apartment, she caught sight of a man in a black hoodie, loitering in front of the McClure house. Ace protectively stepped in front of Katie. When the man noticed them, he fled up the sidewalk. Ace broke into a sprint. "I'll try to catch him," he shouted.

She shivered, even though it was a warm August day. She prayed Ace would catch the stalker and wouldn't get himself killed in the process.

Ace hadn't kept up with his daily jogging since he'd been in West Virginia, so a sudden, unrelenting stitch in his side slowed him down. By the time he rounded the street corner, the hooded man had vanished.

Who was that guy and what was going on? No way his boss had sent in some kind of hit team, knowing Ace hadn't even finished the job yet.

Still, he had to get moving on his plan. His boss wouldn't tolerate heel-dragging. And in a way, these stalkers had already helped him—opening the door for him to step in as the McClures' bodyguard. Perhaps Katie, motivated by fear, would open up to him.

But that wouldn't be easy. He'd seen anger flash in Katie's eyes when he'd challenged her to admit she needed help. Yet she hadn't cracked. He probably should have focused his intentions on her sister Molly, who would have been more than willing to answer his questions without much effort on his part.

And yet something about the plucky redheaded librarian drew him. Maybe it was the genuine grief in her eyes as he described his childhood. Maybe it was the way she was different from other women, almost immune to his magnetism.

But Ace had to admit that he wasn't entirely immune to hers.

3

Mom met them at the door and listened as Katie told her about the stranger.

"Could have been nothing at all," Mom said. "Now you all come in here and get some lunch. You've been working hard."

Mom always looked for the best possible interpretation of any circumstance. Katie wished she'd inherited her mom's optimism, but instead she'd developed a tendency to suspect the worst. Then again, without that cautious instinct, she wouldn't have boldly shouted for everyone to hit the floor in the library, and who knows? Maybe she'd saved someone from getting shot.

Regardless, she determined to give things a cheerier spin when talking to Ace. The poor man probably thought she was one of those "mean girls" who had nothing nice to say to others.

Just as she was about to compliment the chicken salad on croissants, Ace piped up.

"Mrs. McClure, these sandwiches are wonderful. As good as any New York deli."

Mom smiled, pouring him a glass of sweet tea. He took a gulp, then unintentionally pursed his lips before slowly swallowing. Katie had to laugh. The debonair Yankee couldn't hold his sweet tea!

He coughed. "Excuse me, but could I have a glass of water?"

Mom looked befuddled. "Something wrong with your tea? I just brewed it fresh."

Katie silently refilled his glass with water as he struggled to explain. She tried to wipe the smile from her face but found it impossible.

"It's just...sweeter than what I usually drink. I drink unsweetened tea, black coffee...pretty bland stuff, really."

As Katie handed him the glass, he gave her a grateful look. She felt pulled in by those dark-lashed eyes, but briskly looked away. There was a hurt behind them she wanted to know more about. But he wouldn't be around long enough to explain, if the cops could just figure out how to track these men down.

The fact that the guy in the hoodie ran when he saw them was definitely suspicious, but should she tell the cops about him? They might think she was starting to see things, overreacting after the library incident and the home invasion. She decided to keep quiet, hoping it was just a random person loitering for a moment on their sidewalk.

At least they had Ace around.

The day slipped by quickly, with no further incident after the iced tea debacle. Ace had no idea that much sugar could be dumped in tea, and he couldn't figure out how anyone could get used to drinking it that way.

Standing next to an exhausted Katie as they surveyed her now-clean apartment, he felt a fresh sense of pride and accomplishment. He'd done something *right*. And yet his spying and snooping was so wrong. The price of freedom, he told himself for the hundredth time. Once he got done with this job, he'd never see his boss again.

But he would never see Katie McClure again, either.

Glancing at her, he was again surprised by how tall she was. Even as she drooped against the counter, taking the weight off her bad foot, he sensed her hurt ran deeper than an external injury.

"So...did you always want to be a librarian?" he asked.

She blinked rapidly, but didn't look at him. "No."

"You don't like your job?"

"That's not what I said." She brushed bangs from her eyes and fixed him with a weary look—one that was old beyond her years. "I like being a librarian. I'm good at it, and I love the people. But I had other plans. I wanted to be in the FBI like my dad."

He raised his eyebrows, unable to respond. Having done his homework, he was already aware that Sean McClure had been in the FBI and that he had died of an unexpected heart attack at the age of fifty-one. But a woman who wanted to choose an FBI career? He had never run into anybody like Katie.

She frowned at his incredulous look. "What? You don't think I could have done it? Back then, it would've been easy. I practiced shooting. I started taking judo when I was eight. I used to run five miles every morning. I could have done it, Mister...Doubter."

Her prickly exterior faded a bit, revealing a glimpse of a girl who'd desperately wanted to prove herself until her opportunity was snatched away. He lightly touched her arm and was surprised when she didn't recoil.

"I understand what it is to fail to meet expectations—those others put on you or the ones you put on yourself." He shifted his gaze from her teary eyes to the window, struggling to maintain his cool. "I'd better get going. It's already late afternoon."

She followed him outside. "Thank you. But wait—what if they come back at night?"

He had already thought of this angle, but was waiting for her to recognize it.

Fear darkened her eyes. "I know how to use Dad's gun, but haven't gone target shooting for a long time. Maybe...maybe you'd better stick around closer. You can stay in my apartment, if you'd like, since I've moved back over to the house for now. It would save you money, especially since we can't afford to pay you Manhattan wages. That way you could keep an eye out, if you wouldn't mind."

He shrugged, trying to hide his excitement at this inside opportunity. "Of course. It's a great suggestion that makes all kinds of sense. I'll run back to The Greenbrier and check out. I can pick up some food on the way back."

"Goodness, don't bother. Mom always makes enough to feed an army. She'd be happy to have you over."

As Ace slid into the Lexus, he adjusted the rearview mirror and glanced at his smug look. He felt like kicking himself. Faker. Liar. Worthless.

Granny's voice filled his mind. "God knew you before you were even born. Follow after Him and He will lead you on right paths."

That was his problem. He had stopped following God. He wouldn't know a right path if it rose up and punched him in the face.

But he was pretty sure it didn't look like this con-job he was pulling on the McClures.

◦∾⟨Ꝑ⟩∾◦

After telling Mom about Ace's willingness to stay in the garage apartment, Katie trudged into her room and flopped on the bed. She wanted to go for a walk in the woods behind their house, but didn't dare expose herself to whoever might be lurking around.

When she was a teen, Dad had felled several trees to make a clearing in the woods. He surrounded the opening with honeysuckle bushes, forming a haven of sorts. Recognizing Dad's rare effort to build something lasting for his family, they had all pitched in, stringing Christmas lights from tree branches and setting up a fire pit to make it comfy.

Brandon had built a picnic table, and she and Molly had it painted blue. Now the table was covered in a blanket of leaves, sitting unused since last summer.

It always seemed enchanted, that wonderland showcasing

not only the apple green leaves of spring, but the deep golds and russets of fall. When she lost herself in the woods, Katie always gained new perspective.

But now the thought of some man lurking around their home chilled her. What if someone attacked her? She couldn't run or kick. All the joy she used to take in developing her strength and skills had vanished right along with her ability to walk straight.

At least her room overlooked their woodland paradise. She gazed at the trees, fully clothed in summer green. Suddenly, she froze. The man with the black hoodie stood out against the natural backdrop, his binoculars fixed on her.

⁂

On his way to The Greenbrier, Ace's cell phone buzzed. He tapped his hands-free headset and his boss' rough voice nearly blasted his eardrum.

"You found anything yet?"

It was early in the game. Why was he already asking?

"Not yet. These things take time and finesse."

"You better finesse your way right into that stash, Ace. I tapped you for this job because I know how the ladies love you. It should be no problem to extract information from one of those girls."

"I know. I'm working on it." Ace felt like laying on the gas, but it was impossible to do that on these curving mountain roads. "By the way, you want to explain why there's another crew down here working on the McClures? Are those your people?"

Dead silence reigned. Maybe the wireless signal went out? He glanced at his phone. Still had bars.

"Are you *kidding me?*" His boss sounded like he wanted to punch something. Or maybe shoot something.

"It's no joke." Ace filled his boss in on the thugs' appearance at the library. When he mentioned the ransacking at the McClures, his boss lost all control. Ace could almost hear him spitting into the phone.

"You gotta get in there and find that money first. I'm betting Anatoly sent his men down. That Russian—" His boss launched into a string of profanities, some of which were even fouler than the ones Ace had heard in prison. He concluded with, "You'll have to watch your back. But you're finishing this thing. Or you'll be locked up again—I'll make sure of it."

Ace stifled a groan. He was too far gone now. Quitting wasn't an option. He couldn't leave the McClures exposed to those Russian mobsters, and there was no way he was going back to prison. All he had to do was find the stash and he could wake up from this nightmare. His boss' minions would probably settle things with the Russian henchmen once he handed the money over.

The 1.5 million that Sean McClure, FBI agent, had stolen from Anatoly.

He still found it impossible to believe that Sean had risked his family and life to make off with bank heist money. How had he worked it out? Why hadn't his FBI superiors discovered it?

In the years that had elapsed since Anatoly's heist, the mobster had doubtless grilled all his men about the theft, maybe bumping a few off along the way. And yet why had he only recently realized Sean McClure might have taken the money? What had tipped him off?

His boss continued, words tinged with a threatening edge. "I'm coming down in a few days. I want to talk face to face and make sure we understand one another."

After setting up a time and place, Ace hung up and groaned. Tonight he would search the apartment and maybe the garage. His boss had just shortened his timeline. Showing up clueless and empty-handed wouldn't go over well at their meeting.

When he parked, he noticed a text had come through from Katie. She must have gotten his number off his business card. He stared at the screen.

Katie: *Hoodie Man in woods. Do I call the cops!?!*

The text had been sent seven minutes earlier. He texted back, choosing his wording carefully in light of Katie's obvious fear:

Ace: *Is he still there? Don't worry. I will be there soon. Just stay inside.*

Her reply came quickly:

Katie: *He's gone now, from what I can tell. I have the gun. Mom is working on supper. I didn't even tell her.*

He smiled and texted back:

Ace: *Good girl. I'll be there soon. Will knock five times.*

At The Greenbrier, he raced into his yellow-wallpapered suite and began snatching clothes from drawers and tossing them into his open suitcase. As he packed up his bathroom things, he met his own deceitful eyes in the mirror. Had Sean McClure been like him, trapped in an impossible situation? Or had he willingly opened Pandora's box when he decided to steal heist money from a Russian mobster?

Didn't matter. Ace would find the money, if there was money to be found. If not...

He hated to think what Anatoly's men might do to the McClures.

⸎

Katie trailed behind Ace as he combed the woods. Dad's lightweight Sig felt natural in her hands. She had to make time to go shooting, to remind herself of the weight of the trigger pull and the feel of the gun's slight kick. But even now, she was confident she could hit her target, should the need arise.

She was impressed how methodically Ace searched for Hoodie Man. When he finally pronounced the woods abandoned, she took a deep breath of air, trying to slow her shallow breathing.

She dropped onto the picnic table bench, carefully placing the Sig on the bed of leaves in front of her. Ace followed suit, sitting across from her.

He took a long look at her, scanning her face intently. Was he staring at all her freckles? A blush crept up and she propped her face in her hands to hide it, leaning on the tabletop.

Thankfully, he took the hint and glanced up at the sky instead. "Storm moving in, I think."

"For a city boy, that's pretty astute. Usually I can smell them coming."

He grinned. "I remember sticking a hand between our window bars, catching raindrops before they hit the pavement. It does actually rain in the city, you know."

She laughed. "I guess it does."

His focus casually shifted to her lips. When his eyes met hers, they held some kind of unasked question.

Her sister would have rushed to fill the silence, joking and flirting. But she wasn't Molly. And so she waited.

The hush continued, stretching interminably. Finally, he broke it.

"So your dad was FBI, right?"

She nodded.

"Was that hard on you?"

She shifted, fingering the cool metal of the gun. How did she explain that although Dad's long hours hadn't affected her, his bravery had? He had been willing to put his life on the line to protect the people of the United States.

And why had God taken a man like that so early? Sometimes she felt like God enjoyed snatching things from her—her ability to walk properly, her father, her chance for an exciting future...but she couldn't let her mind go there.

"Some jobs require long hours. Dad had one of those jobs. We understood."

His clear eyes filled with pity, something she simultaneously hated and craved. As large raindrops splattered her nose and cheeks, she grabbed the Sig, happy to close the conversation. "We'd better head inside. I'll bet Mom has a warm supper waiting."

4

Katie observed the normally chatty Northerner as he fell silent during their evening meal. Maybe he didn't care for chicken and dumplings, or maybe he was disappointed they hadn't nabbed the man in the woods.

She smiled as he drank the unsweet tea she'd made for him. She had been so tempted to throw in just a tablespoon of sugar—unsweet tea seemed so unnatural—but resisted. Apparently it hit the spot, because he'd asked for another glass.

"Thank you for the meal, Mrs. McClure." Ace rubbed his forehead, like he was exhausted. "I think I'll head over to the apartment and gear up to keep watch tonight." He scraped his plate, placing it carefully on the counter before walking out.

Katie helped Mom clear the table, then cut a slice of key lime pie to take out to Ace. A taste of Mom's famous pie was sure to cheer him up.

He stood outside the apartment in the waning light, tacking a piece of plywood over the open door pane. "I stopped by that hardware store in town and ordered glass for this. Should come in next week. It's standard size."

She was taken aback at his thoughtfulness, which he seemed to be downplaying. "Thank you for doing that." She motioned to the piece of pie. "I'll just put this inside." She scooted around him, through the open door.

His all-black luggage was piled in the corner of her small living room. She snickered when one whopper-sized suitcase caught her eye. For such a brief bodyguard conference, he'd packed even more clothes than a woman would. She could imagine what her brother would say about that.

She set the pie plate on the counter next to his gun, realizing it wasn't the .45 he'd carried earlier today. This one was a nine millimeter, she felt sure. She wondered if it was a Sig Sauer, like her dad's. Gently picking it up, she examined the frame for the brand...

"Put that down!" Ace's deep command echoed in the small apartment. Startled, she returned the weapon to the counter. How dare he assume she was doing something stupid?

She tried to explain. "I just wondered what it was."

Ace gave her a hassled look. "It's a gun, and you shouldn't be handling it."

Anger boiled up. Words exploded from her like fireworks. "I know good and well it's a gun, you dimwit. I just wondered if it's a Glock, a Sig, or a Ruger. I told you I know how to handle guns—you saw me with one today."

Ace crossed his arms. "And you told me you hadn't gone shooting for a while. You can't be casual with firearms, as I'm sure you know."

Now he was lecturing her. Katie raised her chin and tried to stomp out the door , but her awkward gait morphed into a step-drag canter. Regardless, she did succeed in brushing past Ace like he was yesterday's trash.

Once in her room, Katie burst into tears. She already knew she was incapable of doing most of the things she wanted, but to be talked down to like that was insufferable. She wished she could pull a judo flip on Ace or throw a vase at his head.

But a deeper part of her wished she could say the words that would calm his stormy eyes and make him smile. It *had* been foolish to handle someone else's gun. Maybe she should apologize in the morning.

When Molly showed up for her belated supper, Katie emerged briefly to say hello, then skulked back to her room. Like any good sister, Molly followed her. She probed and prodded until Katie gave in, recounting the day's events.

As Katie finished sharing about the gun-touching incident, Molly shocked her by laughing outright. Auburn curls tumbled around her face. "You know what your problem is, don't you? Why, Katie Beth McClure, you're smitten with that Yankee!"

Katie blushed as a wave of realization hit. Why hadn't she seen it? Truth be told, she was downright fascinated with Ace Calhoun.

Molly continued to dispense her sisterly advice. "Right now, the sparks are flying. But you need to figure out if you all have anything in common. He's from New York City, you're from West Virginia. He totes guns, you shelve books. You know Dad and Mom didn't have a lot in common, but Dad was a

Christian and so is Mom." Molly's hazel eyes fixed on hers. "You need to get to know that boy, sis."

Later, as Katie snuggled into her soft, worn sheets, she reread a few chapters of *Little Men*, one of her favorite books by her favorite author, and one that never failed to make her feel calm and happy. As usual, she savored the interactions with Professor Bhaer and his wife, Jo. If only she could find a man like that, someone who loved her just as she was, yet challenged her to be better than she ever thought she could be.

Shockingly, Ace Calhoun came to mind. She snickered. Well, the man certainly didn't hesitate to challenge her, that was for sure.

She hesitantly prayed that she could have more chances to get to know Ace Calhoun…and that God would help her bite her tongue in the process.

⸙

After an uneventful night, Ace joined Katie and Mrs. McClure at the kitchen table for French toast. Must be someone really liked it. He remembered Granny's pancakes, light and fluffy as cotton candy. As he sipped his second cup of black coffee, he turned to Katie, determined to smooth things over from his outburst last night. "You want to go shooting sometime? As you know, I have an extra handgun."

A wide smile stretched across Katie's face, triggering a nearly electric response in him. She had no idea what a knockout she was.

Leaning toward him, she briefly rested her hand on his,

obviously pleased. "I'd love to!"

He tamped down the guilt that rose like bile in his throat. Last night, after going over every inch of Katie's apartment, he'd decided to take a more aggressive tack in gaining access to the McClure home. This shooting scheme was just another step in his plan, a way to ferret out where Sean McClure could have hid the bank money.

He'd found no clues as he'd examined Katie's apartment—right down to the diaries in her bedside table drawer. Apparently, she hadn't nosed into her dad's work much. Her diaries were full of written-out prayers, asking God why she had a limp, why her dad died young, and why she couldn't find a man who would love her for who she was.

In other words, her dream man looked like his exact opposite. Wasn't he just using her for his own ends, like a phony?

This morning, as he stared at Katie's welcoming, Julia Roberts-wide smile, he faltered. He wished he could be that dream man.

The man his granny had prayed he'd grow up to be.

Katie wasn't sure where Ace's magnanimous suggestion to go shooting came from, but she'd take it. First, because she used to enjoy shooting immensely, before *the unfortunate event*, her private nickname for that injurious volleyball game. Second, because Molly had been right. She felt a spark of interest in Ace Calhoun that she'd rarely felt with any other man.

She peeped over her favorite sunset-colored mug, watching him carry on an easy conversation with Mom. There was something about him—not just the chiseled nose and chin, or his striking combination of blue eyes and dark hair. There was something deeper about Ace, something not easily visible on the surface.

She couldn't imagine having a job that would cover a stay at The Greenbrier. Sure, Molly got her in for meals now and again with her employee discount, but she would feel ostentatious paying for even one night at the lavish hotel. And yet here sat a man who took it as a matter of course, who rented a Lexus, and who had more than one handgun.

Her cell phone rang, startling her. Mom grinned and gave her a quick wink. So she wasn't unaware of her daughter's scrutiny of the hired gun.

As Katie picked up, Reba's weary voice filled her ear. "Could you come in today?"

"Um…" Katie glanced over at Ace. What would he do? Stay here and guard Mom? But who would guard her? Oh, well. She couldn't live in fear forever. "Sure. I can come in around ten."

"Oh, honey, that'd be great. We're getting swamped already with all these summer reading activities. Kids bouncing off the walls today." Reba abruptly hung up.

Taking in Mom and Ace's anxious stares, Katie made a public service announcement. "I'm going in to the library today. I'll be fine."

Ace glanced at Mom as if they had some secret understanding. "I'll come along," he said.

Mom nodded. "I have to go into town today anyway, so I won't even be around. It's more important that you get back to your normal life."

How many times had Katie heard that in high school? She never understood how she could get back to her normal life when she was living her new "normal." But she knew better than to sass her mom, who only meant well. She turned to Ace.

"Okay, but you'll just need to stay out of the way. They're really busy." She tried to channel some of last night's irritation with Ace, but found it had almost completely dissipated. The man was winning her over, no doubt about it.

"Will do." He stood and carried their plates to the sink, then returned to tote the milk back to the fridge.

Katie had to admit, this city boy was no slouch around the kitchen. That was more than she could say about most of the guys she'd dated.

⚜

He was going to find that money in the next couple days if it killed him.

As Ace brushed his teeth, he reflected that Katie seemed to be softening toward him. He would try to keep those positive feelings flowing. Maybe he'd launch a barrage of compliments, or touch her elbow repeatedly as he earnestly spoke to her. Those tried-and-true flirting techniques had yet to fail him. But in case of emergency, there was always the old fallback—fake an injury.

It was despicable, this plan. But there was no way around it.

He had to gain access to Sean McClure's things, and the only way in was through Katie.

The library was hopping, as both children and parents disregarded the unwritten keep-it-to-a-whisper rule. Katie jumped right in, entering data from the summer reading forms and guiding children to bookshelves.

Ace seemed content to sit on an extra rolling chair and observe. Reba had only hesitated a moment to let the bodyguard bypass the *No Guns Allowed* restriction posted on the library door. She didn't want to take any chances with a library full of children running around, and Katie was thankful she could focus on her work instead of worrying about masked men.

When she finally glanced at the clock, it was nearly one and they hadn't taken a lunch break. Ace must be starving; he was such a large and well-muscled man. She tried to keep her eyes from wandering to his biceps, which filled out his fitted blue dress shirt in a most impressive way.

She gathered her purse and keys and walked over to him. "I'm so sorry. I totally lost track of time. I have an hour lunch break."

He stood, halting his apparently tireless visual rounds of everyone in the library. He met her gaze. "Sounds good."

"You want to run home and get something to eat? Mom always has sandwich supplies and chips. Or if you're into healthy, I'm sure there's fruit and hummus."

He shot her a radiant smile, and she nearly lost her balance. "I'll eat anything. I'm easy to please."

Reba reluctantly agreed to let them go, her eyes lingering on Ace's holstered guns. Katie prayed there would be no repeats of the other day's armed guest appearance while they were out.

Ace seemed unusually chatty in the car. "Those kids were cracking me up. One of those little boys kept circling the front desk, his eyes glued to my guns."

"It's not every day they see someone like you sitting around. I mean, you do cut an impressive figure." Her cheeks heated and she tried to will the blush away.

He was watching her, but she forced herself to keep her eyes on the road. It was awkward being confined in her small car with such a fine specimen of a man. She struggled to land on a topic of conversation, finally saying the first thing that popped into her head.

"So, were you close to your grandma?"

He stretched his legs, then adjusted his seat so he could keep them fully extended. "I was."

She could tell he was hedging, dancing around something he didn't want to share. Should she keep probing?

Hoping to keep him talking about himself for a change, she said, "So tell me about her. Was she one of those cozy knitting grandmas or one that goes out line dancing?"

To her relief, he laughed. "I don't think they line dance up my way. But she wasn't a knitter, either. To be honest, the main things I associate with my granny are good cooking and going to church."

Katie tried to hide her surprise. "We go, too. You're welcome to come along."

She glanced over and took in his serious look.

Finally, he sighed. "I don't believe in that stuff now."

Something pricked Katie's heart. Yes, she believed in *that stuff*, but did she really believe all of it? If she dug deep and examined her blackest thoughts, she had been angry with God for years. Even as she sang songs in church, read her Bible, and prayed, there was a splinter of doubt that always needled her...that feeling that God had enjoyed keeping her from the life she wanted.

"You look pensive," he said.

"Sorry."

"It's not a bad look. But I do prefer your smile."

She smiled in return for his compliment as she pulled into the driveway. "Thanks. And, Ace?" She pulled out the key and looked full into those disarming blue eyes. "I understand where you're coming from."

◦⤛⤜◦

As Katie dropped her brown sack purse to the couch, Ace noticed a white envelope protruding from an inside pocket. He pointed to it.

"Love letter?" he joked.

She drew her eyebrows together. "I don't know what that is. Reba already gave me my paycheck."

Pulling the envelope out, she gasped. "It's from them—I just know it. It says *To Miss McClure*."

What? That purse had been sitting right there, on the librarians' desk, the entire time. How could anyone have slipped something in? Was Reba in league with Anatoly's thugs? Or had they taken advantage of his one bathroom break and shoved it in then?

Katie ripped into it before he could stop her, tearing the entire end off the envelope. He hoped they hadn't laced it with anthrax or some chemical weapon. Katie's hands shook as she pulled out a crumpled piece of notebook paper and read:

"We're done playing games, Miss McClure. Anatoly wants what's rightfully his. Your family will stay in our sights until you bring us what your daddy stole. You send us a text message at this number when you find something: 212-589-3316. It's untraceable so don't even bother. If we don't hear from you in four days, we will come and find it ourselves."

She slumped to the couch and Ace grabbed the paper, hating that they had threatened her. And now she knew—

"What Dad stole? What are they talking about? And who is Anatoly?" Tears welled in her eyes.

He had to play dumb, but at the same time, this was an opportunity he couldn't afford to pass up.

"I think Anatoly is a famous crime boss in New York—I've read news articles on him." He tried to sound casual. "I remember he pulled off a huge bank heist years ago, but they couldn't pin it on him because the money was never found."

He watched for a reaction from Katie. Did she know more than she let on?

She seemed oblivious. "But what would my dad have to do with that?"

He hesitated for effect. "Your dad was in the FBI. Maybe he was in charge of Anatoly's case?"

She shook her head, straight red hair slipping over her shoulders. "Dad never mentioned an Anatoly."

Time for a direct prod. "But did he keep records of his cases somewhere? Didn't you say he had an office?"

She sat up straighter. "Yes, he had one—it's right down the hall. Maybe we should see if he kept any files."

He extended his hand, helping her up. This threatening note had turned out to be a windfall for him. "Okay, but first let's eat something. You're still shaking."

In the kitchen, Katie slowly assembled one turkey sandwich for herself and two ham and Swiss on rye for him. She loaded a large bag of chips, apples, two water bottles, and a package of Oreos into an antique-looking picnic basket.

She fixed him with a determined look. "Let's eat in the woods at the picnic table. I don't care if they're watching us— I have to get out of the house."

He nodded. "I'm locked and loaded."

"Hang on." She went down to her dad's office. When she returned, she racked the slide on the Sig, fitting it into her belt holster.

He carried the picnic basket as they made their way into the still forest. Shafts of sunlight filtered onto Katie's thick red mane, lighting it afire as she cleaned the table. The silent near-reverence of the clearing felt liberating. It chinked at the invisible armor he'd draped around his heart. He forgot about his mission. He forgot about everything except the light touch of Katie's pale fingers as she handed him his sandwich, a lustrous gleam in her eyes.

An uninvited thought hit him with such surety, he couldn't shake it. Grandma would have loved Katie. She would've called her a "sweet young woman" and urged Ace to pursue her.

It was as if he were being prodded from the grave. Or maybe from God.

He shook his head. Fanciful thinking, indeed. He had one job, and one job only: find the money for his boss so he could move on without a prison threat hanging over him...or even worse, an unspoken death threat. He was fairly certain he'd be taking a long walk off a short plank if he didn't find that money.

As they began to eat, he gently led the conversation in the direction he wanted. "I know that note must have rattled you. Not to cast aspersions on your dad, but he was an FBI agent, and they do know how to keep mum." He waited a moment to let that insinuation sink in.

As it did, her eyes widened. "I know my dad wouldn't lie."

"But what if he tried to protect his family by not telling anyone? What if that money is sitting around somewhere?"

Was he laying it on too heavy? Did he seem too eager?

She sighed. "I suppose I could check some other places, just to be sure. I don't want those cretins 'keeping my family in their sights,' or however they put it."

He nodded. "I can help you."

"Thanks." Her gaze flitted from the trees to the house, then to her half-eaten sandwich, then finally rested on him. "I hate this feeling. What if someone's watching me right now?"

He leaned across the table, touching her hand. "I'm here."

She offered him a brave smile, but continued. "I mean, anything could happen. I can't get away, Ace. I can't run. I hate being so…inept. Of course I'm the perfect target for these goons."

The Oreo seemed stuck in his throat. Her fear was grounded—she couldn't run if those mobsters chased her. He had to distract her.

"Didn't you say you're off work tomorrow? We could go shooting, then nose around some of those possible hiding places. Better to feel like you're proactive, rather than reactive, I always say."

She rested her elbows on the table, obviously relieved. "I shouldn't have to work unless Reba gets desperate. Tomorrow it is. We can go to the range my dad liked." She stood and began tidying up, her long hair swishing like she was in a shampoo ad.

"And maybe after work today, we could check out your dad's office," he added, as if it were an afterthought.

Her gaze sharpened for a split second. He candidly met her eyes, but his insides twisted with the weight of his own treachery. Docile as Katie McClure seemed, he was betting there was a serrated edge to that smooth demeanor. An edge that would push her to take risks for her family.

Risks such as putting her trust in a fake bodyguard like him.

5

Their search of Dad's office hadn't turned up anything. Katie hadn't wanted to let on about the note, so she told Mom they were looking for more ammo—which wasn't entirely untrue. They had emptied every drawer and file, working into the evening. Finally, after a late supper, they had agreed there was nothing to be found and headed to their respective rooms.

The pitch-dark night sky seemed to amplify every little noise outside her window. She was positive someone was creeping around, but the dogs next door were silent, so she finally turned on her box fan around three in the morning and drifted into turbulent dreams.

Reba had asked her to come to the library for a half-day, but she and Ace could hit the shooting range after that. She didn't want to admit it, but being around the buff bodyguard made her feel secure.

Stepping out of her morning shower, she thought about the threatening note she had handed off to him. If she contemplated the scrawled message inside, an icy wedge of fear stabbed at her.

A song from her childhood came to mind—a Bible verse set to music. "When I am afraid, I will trust in Thee." She hummed it to herself, over and over, trying to displace the anxiety. Yes, even more than Ace, she had to trust in God. But that didn't mean she had to drop her guard. Shooting practice would come in handy, giving her confidence to conceal-carry the Sig, at least until the threat blew over.

But she knew it wouldn't blow over until Anatoly's thugs got their money.

Donning her favorite khaki jacket and brown pants, she twisted her hair up and glanced at her reflection. All she needed was a pair of black glasses to scream *Librarian*. If only she could glam it up like Molly. She had a brief image of herself at The Greenbrier restaurant, dressed to the nines, across from Ace in a tuxedo. He would look a little like Cary Grant, she decided.

A knock on her door pulled her back to reality. "You ready?" Ace sounded impatient. "I already got breakfast but we're running late."

She sighed. Ace didn't phrase things like a Southerner. He didn't soften his bluntness or coddle her. He never called her *honey* or *sweetie* like most men did. And yet somehow that made him seem more trustworthy.

She grabbed her purse and slipped into brown ballet flats. She would try not to think of oversized thugs and threatening notes. Today she would focus on the children at the library and rest in the quiet presence of the strong man who watched her every move.

Ace hated to waste more time at the library, but searching the house without Katie would never fly. He could only hope the half-day passed quickly so he could get down to the business he came here for.

He covertly observed Katie as she drove. Her face seemed to radiate a peaceful glow. How did she find that peace in the middle of the storm raging around her? She and Mrs. McClure were still eating regular meals, but his own appetite had dwindled after a late-night follow-up call from his boss. The gist of it was find the money...*or else.*

He wiped sweat from his forehead. It must be ninety degrees in this piece-of-junk car, but it was probably all she could afford. Unbuttoning the sleeves on his yellow Brooks Brothers shirt, he haphazardly shoved them up to his elbows.

The heat served to fuel his frustration. If only Katie would work up her confidence and move to a larger city, she could have a decent-paying job that utilized her obvious people skills. That limp seemed to control her life. No one should let anything control them...trap them.

And yet here he sat, trapped. Controlled by a cruel and wicked man. He stretched his leg and kicked the door, not accidentally.

She shot a glance at him. "You okay? Sorry it's so hot. The A/C hasn't worked for years so the car vents just blow hot air around. You want to open windows instead?"

"Sure." He tried to mellow his tone, but couldn't. What was she doing sitting here with him, trusting him? Why hadn't her mom been more wary of a strange bodyguard, no matter how perfectly his credentials had checked out?

Because Ace was too slick, that's why. His boss had chosen him because of that.

The wind tugged strands from her updo, whipping them around her face. What a contrast she was with the Manhattan up-and-comers he had dated. Those meticulously-coiffed women would have run screaming from this clunker that doubled as a wind tunnel.

Yet Katie merely hummed along, oblivious to the wind...and to how completely she had mesmerized him. He couldn't tear his eyes from that soft freckled skin, those plush lips, and that wild hair.

He had to get it together. He had to finish this job.

She slowed as she pulled into the library parking lot. "My space is taken," she said, turning the wheel and crawling up the rows. "Good grief—all the spaces are taken. I hope there wasn't some event going on that I forgot about."

He pointed to an open area behind the dumpster. "Reba probably wouldn't mind if you parked there, would she?"

Only after she had maneuvered into the tight space did he realize her car would be out of eyesight from the library window. It probably wouldn't be a problem, but he'd be sure to leave early after work and sweep the area.

"Thanks for the help." She grabbed her bag and shot him a warm smile. "Time to go impress some kiddos with your big guns." She winked.

A nearly chemical surge caught him off-guard. In so many words, Katie McClure just let him know she found him attractive. A lesser man would prey on that vulnerability to get what he wanted. And today, Ace was that lesser man.

Children begged for another story as Katie finished reading the final chapter of *My Father's Dragon* aloud. She pointed them to the next book in the series, in sore need of a stretch and a snack.

"Thank you so much." One lingering mother patted her back before hustling her children to their next summer activity. Katie returned to her chair, noticing Ace wasn't positioned in his usual spot. Maybe he had taken a snack break himself.

She imagined what it would be like without her loyal bodyguard around. Presumably, as soon as the cops caught up with those thugs, Ace would high-tail it back to New York City. He had given her note to the police in hopes they could analyze the handwriting and trace the phone and track down Anatoly's henchmen.

Grabbing her purse, she headed to the bathroom to re-twist her hair and apply lip gloss. She should have done that upon arrival at the library, but the kids had nearly attacked her, begging her to start reading early. It did feel nice to be loved.

Leaning in toward the mirror, she tried to observe her reflection dispassionately. Clear green eyes, now easily visible because she'd pinned back her bangs. A brand-new flush to her usually pale cheeks. An upward tilt to her lips and only a slight crease in her forehead, which told her that even though she was stressing over that death-threat note, something was keeping her afloat.

That something was Ace. She wanted to kick herself. It needed to be God, not some dude. But what a dude he was. She couldn't wait to get home and change, pick up the Sig, and hit the range. Ace could probably share all kinds of shooting tips with her.

She moved to dodge a woman entering the bathroom, then froze as a boom louder than thunder ripped through the air.

This time she wasn't the one who gave the warning. "Hit the floor!" Ace's deep shout bounced over rows of books as he jogged toward her. She let the bathroom door close fully, but wasn't able to take a step before Ace tackled her, pinning her to the ground.

"Shh. Wait."

"What was that?" She tried to slow her breathing, even though she felt like she was hyperventilating.

"I said *shh*." He released his grip on her wrists, so tight it would probably leave bruises. "Stay put. Sounded like an explosion."

"An *explosion*? I have to check on the children! And Reba! And—"

"You'll do no such thing. I am phoning the police. You aren't going to move until I figure out what's going on." He pulled her to a sitting position. His eyes were dark with concern. "Will you stay here until I come back?"

"You can't leave me! You're my bodyguard!" She probably sounded like a whining child.

He pushed her hair aside and leaned in toward her ear. The proximity of his breath, his masculine smell, and his deep, reassuring voice nearly unleashed her brimming tears.

"I'm not going to leave you alone, Katie." His rough fingers lightly grazed her neck as he shifted her hair back over her shoulders. "I promise."

She settled against the wall, determined to be strong. Some kind of FBI agent she would have made, nearly crumpling into tears in the face of a loud blast.

As Ace went to check things out, she began to pray there would be no more explosions.

For the first time, she allowed herself to entertain the possibility that the bank heist money could have fallen into Dad's possession. If it had, didn't she have a responsibility to find it and stop this madness?

Maybe it wasn't even Dad's doing. What if his partner, Jim Chrisman, had been dirty? He could have hidden the money somewhere. Strangely enough, Jim's life had also been cut short, undetected late-stage cancer taking him a year before Dad. She remembered Jim's jokes about her red hair every time he came to go fishing on Dad's boat.

There was an idea: they could search the boat. She hadn't been to the marina in years, but Mom maintained the membership for Brandon, since Dad had left his boat to him.

She was tired of being a target. It was time to go proactive, like Ace had said.

❦

Staring at the smoldering, twisted remains of Katie's car, Ace wished he could beat himself up.

Bomb-sniffing dogs had swept the parking lot and the library and it became apparent that only one charge had been set—directly under Katie's car.

He now realized it was no accident that all the parking spots had been taken this morning. He cringed, imagining Anatoly's men as they hunched in multiple cars, observing Katie and him. After he'd obliviously walked her into the library, those punks had probably planted that C4 charge and later remote-detonated it.

At least they had blown the heap after the kids left the library, and before they had walked to the car at closing time. That told Ace they weren't ready to kill Katie yet. They still believed she would find the money.

After sharing his suspicions with the police sergeant, he walked toward the library, but the sergeant motioned him up the hill. "They've been evacuated. That way."

Ace followed the man's pointing finger up the incline the building was situated on. On Main Street, a cluster of library evacuees huddled in front of the bank. He easily spotted Katie's towering red head and rushed to her side.

"What happened, Ace? Before they moved us over here I looked out the window—where's my car?"

There was no way to soften the truth. As he explained that her car had been the target of an explosive charge, she began to shake violently.

Instinctively, he pulled her close and smoothed her forehead as he would a feverish child. "Shh. It's okay. It's going to be okay." He tried to ignore how perfectly her body snuggled into his side. She was tall, but the right kind of tall.

A coconut scent wafted from her hair and he tried to focus. "I'll get you home, don't worry."

She pulled back, resting her still-shaking hands on his chest. But determination filled the steady gaze she leveled on him. "No. We're not going to go slinking home. I'll phone Mom and see if someone can pick us up, but we're going to get your rental car and take a little trip to our storage unit and some other places. It's high time we started hunting for that money so I can protect my family."

6

Mom picked them up in her small Toyota, wiping at her eyes the entire trip home.

"It's okay. I'm okay." Katie kept up a stream of reassurances, but Mom's uncharacteristic silence hung like a weight in the car. When Esther Sue McClure's bubble of cheer was popped, the only way she could deal with it was to retreat into herself. It had happened only once before that Katie remembered, for the entire year following Dad's death. She had prayed Mom would never have to go through such grief again.

But then again, maybe Dad's decisions had brought these mobsters to town. Had he stolen that money, regardless of the heartache it might cause his family? She couldn't believe that.

She felt an urge to call her brother. Maybe Dad had mentioned something to him? It had been too long since she'd seen Brandon's familiar red-bearded face on Skype. She would call him tonight.

But for now, she and Ace had work to do.

After a brief lunch, Katie called Mom's best friend to come

and stay with her a while. If anyone could offer wisdom in a tough situation, it was Jeannie Young. Jeannie had lost her son in Afghanistan, yet amazingly, her faith in God had only grown stronger since.

She pocketed keys to the storage building and boat. Mom shot her a questioning look from the couch.

"I thought I'd show Ace the marina while he's here, take a break from all the library stuff." It wasn't the whole truth, but Mom didn't need to hear about Dad's possible corruption right now. "My cell phone is charged if you need me. I'm feeling fine, Mom—I promise."

Mom offered a resigned nod. "Yes, you might as well get out of the house."

As Katie sank into the cozy Lexus seat, Ace remained quiet. His eyebrows furrowed as if the weight of the world sat on his shoulders.

She was beginning to feel like the designated situation-lightener. "Don't worry. You did your job and made sure I was all right. And I am."

He shot her a dubious look. "But you shouldn't be. Someone blew up your car, Katie. Doesn't that bother you?"

She sat back, stung by his harshness. "Well, of course it does. But what can I do about it, besides what we *are* doing?"

He ran a hand through his hair, creating dark, disheveled spikes. She was possessed by the strangest urge to reach over and smooth it back down.

He continued. "What I mean is, aren't you worried about losing your life? You only get one shot at it, you know."

So that was what was on his mind. "I know where I'm going when I die, so I'm not scared. Of course I want to live a long time—don't we all? And yes, we only get one go-round on this life. So I want to make the most of it." She paused, letting the reality of her words sink in. Yes. She wanted to make the most of this life God had given her, not cower around wishing she could be Molly or anyone else.

He didn't say another word as she directed him to the storage facility. Once there, he pulled into the empty lot and parked outside the barbwire fence. She took Mom's key and unlocked the gate.

When she opened the double doors to their unit, she peered into the jam-packed space and apologized. "Sorry this is so full of junk. Knowing Mom, we probably still have bins of baby clothes in here."

It was stuffy as all get-out as she tried to maneuver deeper into the building. Ace hung back, propping the doors open and taking a long, measuring glance around. "Tell me where your Dad's things are."

Stumbling around bed frames, lamps, and camping supplies, she finally managed to locate Dad's boxes. She swept her arm out. "His things are from about here on over."

He nodded and pointed to the left. "How about you take that half, I'll take this?"

They pawed through box after box for over an hour. She wished she'd packed something to drink in the parching heat. She was about to suggest they hit the nearby Wendy's when his phone rang.

He checked the caller, then motioned to his car. "I have to take this."

As he strode outside, she couldn't help but wonder. Was it some kind of private call from a girlfriend?

Minutes slowly ticked by. The combination of stifling building, thirst, and repressed shock from the morning's car bombing began to weigh on her. Things began to get dark around the edges and she felt herself slipping from the box she sat on.

Abruptly, Ace's strong hands gripped her, shifting her entire body into his massive arms. "I'm taking you out to the car." He carried her to the leather car seat, where he positioned her with her head over her knees.

As he started the engine, air-conditioning hit her face full-blast. She gasped and nearly clobbered her head on the dashboard.

"Take it easy," he said, gently pushing her head down again. "You nearly passed out. I'm going to find something to drink for you."

He seemed to know where he was going, whipping around the winding mountain roads like a native. Good thing she didn't get car-sick, like Molly. Pulling into the Wendy's drive-through, Ace barked orders for four waters. At the next window, he practically threw a twenty-dollar bill at them, then grabbed the bottles and passed one to her. She eased into a sitting position.

"Drink this, slowly. And breathe deep," he said.

She did as told and started to feel a bit refreshed. Not to

mention, utterly humiliated. She was so weak.

"I'm so sorry—" she started.

"Don't apologize. It was my fault. Paid too much attention to my phone call and not enough to you."

"Who was it?" Why did she feel the need to pry?

"My boss." He didn't elaborate, just sucked down half his water bottle.

"So sorry—I'll bet you need to head on back to New York. And here you are stuck in West Virginia." She should dip into her savings to help Mom pay him for his services.

He took another gulp of water and turned to her. Those blue eyes pulled her in, like specks of ocean in land-locked Hemlock Creek. He stretched out a hand and cupped her cheek.

"You have more color. That's good. I didn't realize you had so many freckles until you blanched out back there." He gave her a half-smile. "Let's go back to the building and finish up. You're a trooper for doing this, especially when we're getting nowhere." His voice roughened. "And by the way, you have a habit of apologizing for things you don't have any control over. I don't want you ever to apologize to me again."

"Never?" She grinned. "Must mean I'm perfect."

He gazed at her just a second too long. "It's not that much of a stretch."

This was getting too stupid. How dare his boss call him in the middle of the day, knowing he was probably with Katie? Not only that, but he had simply repeated his earlier threats, as if those hadn't come through loud and clear with the last call.

Katie *was* a trooper, going back into the storage building. The relentless heat had completely plastered his oxford shirt to his back, forcing him to strip down to his T-shirt.

And for what? A search for money that probably wasn't there.

Now they'd taken another half-hour to rummage through the remainder of Sean's boxes and even his T-shirt was soaked. Katie looked okay but was still peaked, even as she sipped at her water. He needed to get her out of here.

He stretched and made a proclamation. "That's enough. We've been through every box. There's nothing to find here."

She handed him the building keys in an exhausted silence, then limped out to the car. He followed, turning on the engine so she could sit in the air-conditioning while he locked up.

She was speaking on the phone when he returned. She wrapped up her conversation, turned off the phone, and explained. "I called Reba. She's hanging in there, but she's closing the library for the rest of the week. So we can take our time checking Dad's boat. Thanks so much for doing all this." She smiled, at first hesitantly, then that blinding-wide smile that made him feel like a hero.

Couldn't be further from the truth. Her hero was a villain.

Dad had been a member of the Sutton Lake Marina since Katie had turned twelve. His Cabin Cruiser boat, the *Vixen*, was the one thing he had splurged on for himself with his earnings. At least she hoped it had been his earnings.

She treasured memories of summer nights she'd camped on the deck in her sleeping bag, picking out constellations as the boat lightly bobbed beneath her. Back then, she'd felt like she could do anything, be anyone.

After her accident, she'd stopped visiting the *Vixen*, mostly because she felt off balance and feared she'd pitch overboard like a klutz.

Again. Fear. She had begun to see it for what it was, to name it. This frantic race to find the bank money was driving her to overcome those fears...that, and the confidence of having Ace Calhoun by her side.

As they stepped onboard, she took the steadying hand he offered, glancing at his face. His Yankee candor seemed to have been replaced with reticence since the explosion. It was like he had gone inward, and she really wished she knew how those gears in his head were churning.

She fiddled with the rusty lock on the cabin door, finally jiggering it open. They stepped into the small space that smelled faintly of mildew. Mom had never cared much for sailing, so it hadn't been cleaned for a while.

"We need to get looking or we'll melt in here." She propped the door open, then gestured to the cabinets by the small refrigerator. "You check the right side, I'll check the left. Or should I say, you check starboard and I'll check port."

He cracked a smile. "Well, aren't you all nautical?"

"I'd forgotten how much I love this. I used to wish I could

live on a houseboat, like MacGyver."

"You watched that show?"

"Just the re-runs."

"I didn't know you were a retro TV girl. I'm a big *A-Team* fan, myself."

They fell into a companionable silence as they began to plunder the cabinets.

Bypassing cans of Spam and pork and beans that were probably three years expired, she pulled up a zippered pouch. "Hey, what's this?"

He was by her side in a moment. His cologne made it hard to concentrate, and she couldn't ignore the way his damp T-shirt draped his muscles. Seriously, the guy could probably beat up three men at once.

After unzipping the pouch, she pulled out folded bank statements and handed him half of them. She felt somewhat traitorous sharing them with someone outside the family, but it was for the greater good.

They read over the papers, finally coming to the conclusion that nothing looked amiss. No out-of-the-ordinary deposits or strange payments had been made.

"It's hopeless." She yanked out another drawer. The heat was so smothering, she had the ridiculous—and inappropriate—urge to strip to her unmentionables and jump in the lake. "Let's go on deck and get some air," she suggested instead.

Outside, Ace didn't hesitate to sprawl out on the warm wood deck, and she carefully lowered herself to join him. But it only took a few moments to realize the blinding sun was going to scald her pale skin. Ace probably couldn't feel it—he had that skin color that seemed to maintain a perpetual tan. She struggled back to her feet. "We might as well get going. Mom's probably working on supper soon and I don't think there's anything here."

"Let's jump in first."

Had he read her mind? It was so hot...

"We can't go home all wet—" she started.

But he had already begun stripping off his T-shirt. He laid his holstered guns on the deck, then boosted himself over the back railing and began to doggie-paddle in the dark lake. He grinned up at her.

"Come on in—the water's fine!" He splashed water on the deck.

How could she resist?

She carefully slid off the port side and did a butterfly stroke to him. She'd forgotten how swimming seemed to erase her limp.

Good grief. She would have never guessed a couple weeks ago that she'd be swimming in Sutton Lake with a personal bodyguard. Especially not with one who looked a whole lot like Superman.

"Are we friends?" The question popped out before she could stop it.

"Of course." He floated languidly, drops of water flecking his sleek chest.

"Good." His companionship had almost been like a security

blanket these past few days.

She dove into the cool water, paying no attention to the sopping blouse and pants that weighed her down. She felt like a carefree kid again.

Boldness filled her and she voiced something she'd been curious about. "So…Ace is an interesting name. Is that your real name?"

He swam closer, his look unreadable. Why had she felt compelled to ask that? She did a few strokes backward, wishing she could vanish.

But his lips curled into a smile. "Yes, believe it or not, it's real. My dad was heavy into baseball. 'Ace' is a term for the best starting pitcher on a team."

"So did you play baseball?"

"Only a little. I wasn't the best at it and I surely wasn't a pitcher. My dad came to one game and as I recall, he left early."

Such disappointment for a little boy. These candid glimpses into Ace's childhood explained who he was more clearly than his often-enigmatic actions.

His smile widened. "But Granny told me 'Ace' can also mean a champion; a master. She prayed that way—that I would become a champion for God."

"I like that." She swam closer. "Sounds like you actually do believe in God."

"I did, as a kid. Asked Jesus into my heart and all that. Granny's prayers carried me along for a while, but then when I was a teen, it became blindingly clear that God didn't seem to be on my side. Then Granny died. It was kind of downhill from there."

She wished she had pithy words of wisdom and restoration to offer, but she had been struggling for years to believe that God loved her and wanted the best for her. So many times it didn't seem like it. Maybe Ace needed to talk to Mom's friend Jeannie—and maybe she did, too.

Ace looked at the sky, then at his waterproof watch. "It's getting late; we'd better get back. I know your mom will be worried."

The moment was lost. But he was right—Mom would worry if they didn't show up soon.

After he climbed back onboard, he helped pull her up. Strangely, she didn't even feel self-conscious about her clothing-laden weight, possibly because she was hyperaware of the secure feeling of her hands in his. His long fingers were surprisingly rough, which appealed to her more than she would have guessed.

They lowered onto the deck benches for a few minutes to dry off so they wouldn't soak the Lexus interior. The waning afternoon sunshine felt just right. She wished she could live in this bubble of light and warmth forever.

Reality intruded as her cell phone buzzed.

"Hello?"

"Katie, where are you?" Molly's voice had a desperate edge to it.

"We're fine. I'm just showing Ace the *Vixen*."

"What? So let me get this straight: your car was bombed into oblivion, but for some reason you two decided to be-bop on over to Sutton Lake? Good grief, sis. You could've let me know.

Didn't you get my texts?"

"I didn't see them—we were busy. And you know me, a real be-bopper." She tried to control a snicker. "We're heading home now. Don't wait up for supper."

Molly huffed. "We won't. I have to get going but I wanted to see my thankfully-still-alive sister before I went out tonight."

"Who you going out with?"

There was an unusually long pause. "Someone you wouldn't know."

Katie's eyebrows shot up. It wasn't like Molly to be cagey about her illustrious dates. "I wish you'd stick around and tell me more about him."

"No time. Maybe another day. But stay safe, okay? That bodyguard better be earning his keep."

As she hung up, Ace stood, helping her to her feet. Near the car, he surprised her by crossing to her door first and opening it. He hadn't done that before.

"Why, thank you." She smiled. "I see you have excellent manners."

"Could be your Southern ways are rubbing off on me."

A zing of hope shot through her chest. She tried to tamp it down, but she couldn't erase a very clear picture that formed in her mind. Ace Calhoun, wearing a plaid shirt and jeans, tromping out to the Christmas tree farm with her family on their yearly tree hunt. Where did that come from? How could he ever fit in here?

As she watched him struggle to squeeze his still-damp body into his dry dress shirt, Ace grinned, and that last domino of hesitancy she had toward him toppled.

The truth was, she'd never met a man who fit so well with *her*. But was he so far gone from God he wouldn't ever come back? She'd always wanted to marry a strong Christian—stronger than her, at least.

It almost felt like something was propelling her toward Ace, something bigger than what she could see or understand. She would begin praying about her mixed feelings in earnest. But one thing she was increasingly sure of: Ace Calhoun was a decent man.

Ace ignored the long red strands of hair whipping around Katie's head. He ignored her contented smile and that glow she seemed to bask in, even after a tedious day in which her car had been blown to smithereens by C4 explosives, to say nothing of the hours she'd spent searching for hidden money with him, nearly passing out in the process.

The storage building had been a bust. The boat had been a bust. He was trying not to show his disappointment, but sometimes it seemed Katie saw right past his smiles into some part of himself he preferred to hide.

What would she think if she ever knew his real motive for staying here?

Stealing a glance at her as she leaned into the seat, relaxed and nearly dozing, he gripped the wheel harder. The truth was, his biggest motive for staying in Hemlock Creek sat right beside him.

7

A much-calmer Mom welcomed them at the door. She didn't bother to ask about their damp clothing. "Come in, come in," she said. "Ham biscuits and gravy coming right up."

The comfort food hit the spot, but Katie feared the exhaustion of the day must have shown on her face.

Mom kissed her head. "You're my sweet baby girl. I'm so thankful you weren't hurt." A warm teardrop slid onto her hair. "Oh, and your brother wants you to call. I didn't tell him what happened to your car."

Funny—she and Brandon always had some kind of uncanny connection, even though they didn't always see eye-to-eye. Even miles apart, he seemed to have an instinct for when she was in need of some big-brother boosting.

"Don't let me stop you," Ace said. "I need to get back over and get some shuteye myself."

She nodded, unable to articulate her gratefulness for his presence at the library, his willingness to go on her wild goose chase for the money, and his talking her into an impromptu but much-needed swimming excursion.

As Mom hummed, scrubbing out her cast-iron skillet, Katie slowly and deliberately covered his hand with her own. When his eyes met hers, questioning, she took a deep breath. "Thank you," she whispered.

For once, it seemed he had nothing to say. He just sat there, his covered hand resting on the wooden tabletop.

Finally, as Mom swung around to wipe down the table, he murmured, "You're one in a million, Katie McClure."

Katie swiped on a bit of powder before Skyping Brandon, lest her natural blush become apparent. She wanted to talk about Dad, not about her bodyguard, who had admittedly set her heart aflutter.

He picked up quickly, giving her a close-up view of his full red beard but not much else.

"Hey, bro—pull that phone back a little!"

He laughed, rearranging his phone camera. "Just wanted to give you the full river-guide mountain-man effect, sis."

"Scary."

"Well, you're looking good. But what's the deal with Mom hiring a bodyguard? I feel like she's only telling me blips of information, like I can't handle the truth."

Knowing her brother's tendency to get overheated, she started at the beginning, explaining the library intrusion, the apartment break-in, the stalker, and finally, as the pièce de résistance, the car bomb. With each event, his eyes widened and his ruddy face grew a shade darker. When she stopped for breath, he exploded.

"I swear I will come back there and I will kill those people! They bombed your car?! I swear I will contact some of Dad's FBI friends! I'm hopping the next plane!"

She used her most soothing voice, trying to talk him down and redirect his attention.

"No need to come back—that's what the bodyguard is for. Plus, the police are on the case. And I actually wanted to ask you about the FBI stuff. Did Dad talk much to you about his friends, or maybe any particular cases?"

Brandon paused, taking a swig of his ever-present can of Dr. Pepper. The flame in his cheeks died down a little. "Let's see. All he ever really mentioned was his partner Jim, because he was always coming over to go fishing, you know? I mean, Dad didn't talk about specific cases. But I do remember him saying they should've done an autopsy on Jim. I think he didn't buy that late-stage cancer explanation for his death. Dad wanted to look into things, as I recall. But it was too late, because Jim had already been cremated, like his will directed."

Dad's suspicions could have been founded. What if Anatoly had killed Jim because he was connected with that bank heist case? And what if...Katie gasped, forgetting she was on camera.

"Sis, what's going on? You're white as a sheet."

She described the note to him, and he jumped to the same conclusion she had.

"So this Anatoly might have killed Jim, then taken out our own dad. For a bank stash that's gone missing." His green-gold eyes darkened. "Sis, I feel like I need to be there with you. Where's Molly? Is she safe?"

"She doesn't seem to be a target right now for some reason. Seems like they've honed in on me."

"Yeah, that doesn't make sense. But if I were there, I could divert attention...then meet those punks with a rocket launcher or something."

She laughed. "Brandon, this isn't one of your shooter video games. This is real life. And I have a bodyguard."

He leaned in, winking. "Now *him* Molly told me about. Tall, dark, and handsome—that about cover it?"

Sighing, she decided to play along. "Yup. Undeniably handsome and nice."

Brandon crinkled his nose, something he did when he was unsure of the situation. "You be careful. Maybe you can't even trust him."

"I can. He's already protected me from danger a couple of times. Why would he do that if he was some kind of mobster?"

"I don't know. But I watch a lot of murder mysteries. It's always the last one you suspect."

"No one's been murdered. Well, at least no one we're sure of."

"Let's keep it that way," he said.

As the morning light trickled in through the white wooden blinds, Ace groaned. His boss was showing up at three this afternoon. Ace had arranged to meet him at the overgrown, ramshackle warehouse he'd noticed on the way to the storage facility.

Before then, he had to wheedle out of Katie any remaining hiding places and search them. Then he could say with confidence the money was nowhere to be found in the McClure household. Surely his boss would take his word for it and leave them alone.

Wouldn't he?

There were no guarantees. This whole business was dicey, from start to finish.

He took extra care as he got dressed—placing one gun in a hip holster, one in an ankle holster, and a small Ruger .380 in a belly band, just in case. He slid a throwing knife into a leg sheath, then slipped on his neck chain that concealed another knife. He would be ready if his boss had any funny business in mind.

He put on a looser-fitting oxford shirt and pants, hoping to project a relaxed vibe while covering his mini arsenal. Striding out into the pale morning light, he followed the path to the McClures' front porch and knocked. Smells of fresh coffee, cinnamon, and nutmeg assailed him as the door swung open.

Molly, dressed in a fitted skirt that accentuated her curves, stood inside the door. Her red platform heels boosted her to his chin height. She draped her arms around him in a loose hug. He automatically stepped back so she wouldn't bump into the weapons on his chest. Could the woman scream *available* any louder?

"Aren't you looking dapper this morning?" She grinned,

taking stock of him from head to toe. "And what are you two up to today?"

Katie emerged from the kitchen, hair tossed into a loose, off-kilter knot. She wore what looked like a boy's Pac-Man T-shirt and acid-washed jeans. Could the sisters be more different?

Katie sipped at her steaming mug. "I thought of one last place we could check. Come on in and have some breakfast. Mom picked up some real maple syrup this time around." She winked.

He nodded, thankful for her lighter demeanor. Molly's heated stare was making him uncomfortable. Since when did a beautiful woman's attention bother him in a bad way? Since Katie, that's when.

As they joined Mrs. McClure at the table, Molly lathered butter on her French toast and jabbed her fork in the air. "Well, you two be careful, whatever you're doing. It's ridiculous that some freak is trying to kill my sister. I swear to you, if I knew how to use guns, I would be dangerous!"

"Probably why Dad never taught you," Katie murmured.

He nearly choked on his coffee. He'd never met a librarian with such a wicked sense of humor.

After Molly swirled out of the kitchen with her usual flair, Mom stood, excusing herself. "I'm going to a Bible study with Jeannie this morning. It's been too long since I've made time for one."

"Maybe I'll go with you sometime...after things calm

down," Katie said. She really did need some accountability.

Mom nodded, giving them a winsome smile. "Stay safe today."

The moment they were alone, Katie lowered her voice. "I stayed up last night thinking about hiding places. Dad sometimes went to the attic, I remember. It's just a crawlspace, really, but there might be something up there."

He nodded. "Good idea. We'll check it out. By the way, I have to head over to town later to pick up that glass panel for your door. Shouldn't take me long. I've lined up for a police patrol unit to sit outside your house starting at two-thirty. They'll stay until I get back."

Leaving her *alone*? He was just casually taking off? She drilled her gaze into his. It didn't take him long to get the message.

"Katie, I wouldn't leave you alone unless I was sure you'd be okay. You have the Sig. You'll have a patrol car outside."

"What if they come through the woods, into the back door?"

"Sit in the living room, where you can get out fast. Lock all the doors. Your mom should be back by then, right? So you won't be completely alone."

She may as well be. Mom was barely better than Molly in an emergency. She had a habit of passing out when her kids bled. The time Brandon sliced his finger with a razor, Katie had been the one who drove him to the E.R.—on her learner's permit. And forget about guns. Mom had no interest in handling one, though she was admittedly handy with her Emeril kitchen knives.

"It's okay," she said, mentally talking herself down. She was not going to be paralyzed with fear. After all, someday Ace would have to leave them—maybe someday soon. If only those cops would track down Anatoly's thugs, maybe the McClures could start to get back to normal.

He gave her a concerned look, but she ignored it.

"We'd better check the attic while Mom's gone." She clomped down the hall, not caring if she looked as unwieldy as a lame elephant. Grabbing a stepstool from Dad's office, she placed it under the attic door and tried to grab at the dangling rope pull. It was just a little too high.

"Allow me." Catching up to her, he offered a slight flourish and a bow.

She shrugged, stepping aside.

He climbed on the stool, pulling the rope and easing the built-in ladder down to the floor. "Are you able to climb up?"

Heat rose in her cheeks. "I'm not handicapped. Just lame. Of course I can get up there." In reality, she had never gone upstairs before and had no idea if her bum foot would hold her weight.

Noting his apprehensive look, she continued. "In fact, I'll head up first." Clinging to one step at a time, she slowly made her way to the top. Once inside the rectangular opening, she screwed in the light bulb to illuminate the tight space. Moving to the side floorboards, she motioned to him, trying not to ponder how she'd ever get back down.

After placing a couple guns on the floor, he climbed up. She tried not to notice as he contorted to squeeze his wide upper body through the narrow opening. Once he was settled on the opposite side, his clean, cedar scent drifted her way. His dress shirt looked rumpled and his hair did, too.

He smiled, his face only half-lit by the dim bulb. "Let's get to work," he said.

But his lingering smile said something else.

They had gone through three bins stuffed with Christmas paraphernalia Mom had probably forgotten she owned. There was only one left.

Ace dug into it, retrieving a worn leather baseball mitt and baseball. "What's this?"

She leaned in for a closer look. "This was probably the baseball stuff Dad gave Brandon. But Brandon never used it—he was born to play soccer, he said. Tough head and all that."

He laughed, fingering the laces. "This is really old-school. Wouldn't my dad love to see this!"

A brainstorm hit her. "I can ask Brandon, but I know my brother, and he couldn't care less about those things. I think you'd be welcome to take it all."

Resting the mitt and ball in his lap, he plunged an arm into the tissue-paper packed bin, retrieving a plastic bag containing a pile of baseball cards. "These too, you think?"

"Oh sure. Hang on—let me text Brandon."

She did, and just as she suspected, received a quick reply:

Brandon: *No problem, give them to the bodyguard. Just symbolic of how little Dad cared about my preferences. Now someone else can enjoy that junk.*

Not exactly eloquent, but honest. "They're all yours," she said.

Nodding, Ace began to pull the tissue paper out. "Looks like this is it…whatever this is at the bottom…" He extracted an oversized purple stuffed panda bear.

"Poopsie!" she exclaimed.

"Excuse me?"

"I mean, that's Poopsie. My purple panda Poopsie. I wondered where he went!" She grabbed the stuffed animal, dust sifting into the air around them. "Dad won him for me at the fair one year. Molly was so jealous that she didn't get one. She made Brandon win her a real goldfish instead, then it wound up dying a week later."

He laughed. A timer on his watch beeped and he anxiously glanced at it. "Sorry, but I need to get moving. The police unit will be showing up any minute now. And I want to help you get down the stairs, even though I know you can probably do it yourself. Am I right in thinking you want Poopsie to accompany you?"

She grinned. "Sure thing."

By the time Mom came in asking about the police car, the attic was closed up and Ace was heading out the door. He waved, promising to return as soon as he could.

It was only then she let it sink in: there was no bank heist money in the house. Maybe there never was any money. What kind of daughter was she to suspect her father stole it in the first place?

8

The crumbling roof on the faded stucco building looked ready to collapse. Ace was glad he was the first to show up, so he could better examine the layout. Kicking open the splintered wooden door, he saw he wasn't the first to use this place for nefarious purposes. Beer cans, cigarette butts, and a moldy mattress decorated the interior.

After checking the large room, he situated himself toward the back, near a window with no glass. He could bail out that way if he had to, even though it would be quite a drop into the creek below. He had just finished checking his guns when the door burst open.

His boss was alone, or so it seemed. Peering out the front, Ace could only see one black car. Probably had a driver inside, maybe one or two extra gunmen at the most.

"Ace Calhoun. My favorite ex-inmate. How ya doin'?"

He hated the false charm this man always showed. From his too-toothy grin to his all-American good looks, he was a total fake.

Fake enough to fool the FBI, in fact. And his partner, Sean McClure.

"Jim." He nodded.

"You been enjoying time with that McClure redhead? Always a bit of a spitfire, that one. Kind of nosy about my visits to her dad's boat. Good ol' Sean, wouldn't he roll in his grave if he saw me alive? He was so sure someone had whacked me."

Ace's stomach turned at the casual way Jim Chrisman spoke of his deceased FBI partner. He was becoming more and more convinced that Sean hadn't been in on the theft.

Jim continued. "You searched that boat, didn't you? I told you where I put it. You check there?"

Ace uncrossed his arms and dropped them to his sides, ready to draw and fire if he had to. "Sure did. One of the first places I looked. It wasn't in the built-in bench."

He braced himself for Jim's wrath, but it didn't come. Instead, an ominous silence fell. The calm before the storm?

Jim smiled even wider. "No problem. I take it you've searched the house?"

"In its entirety."

He stood watchful, waiting for Jim to give some kind of signal. It would be easy enough for his boss to cut his losses and have him killed right here.

Jim stalked closer and Ace recoiled. The man laughed. "Cool your jets. Didn't I spring you from jail? I'm your savior. Now you *are* gonna pay me back. Out of the goodness of my heart, I've decided to give you a couple more days. I'm staying over at The Greenbrier, keeping a close eye on that piece of work, Molly. That one grew up *real* nice."

Ace wanted to punch his lights out.

Jim smirked. "That hurt your feelings, Calhoun? Well, try this on for size. You don't hand me the money in two days, and I'm gonna get cozy with the grieving widow McClure. Esther Sue always did have a soft spot for me, and I'm sure she'd be glad if I came out of—" here he offered air quotes— "'government hiding.' I remember all those nights we sat around the family bonfire, unburdening our hearts to one another." He grunted. "Ours could be a marriage made in heaven. By the way, she *will* marry me, whether she wants to or not. Now, I can't actually say what might happen to those sisters if they get in my way. And the brother...well, he never liked his dad much. Maybe he needs a new one?"

Before he could stop himself, Ace slammed both fists into Jim's chest, sending the shorter man reeling. "You're going to stay out of their lives," he breathed.

Immediately, two armed men entered the room, blocking the door. Jim coughed.

"Don't get fresh with me. I will not get out of their lives, or out of yours, until I have that stash. I know it's around because I hid it myself. No way Sean could've spent all that, and it's not in his accounts. You are going to get to it before Anatoly does, or you'll die trying."

There was no choice. Either he would be the bad guy or Jim would, and he couldn't stomach Jim getting anywhere near the McClures.

"Two days," he agreed.

Jim rubbed at his chest, obviously sore. "I'll see you back here at the same time. And, hey—at our next get-together? My men won't be so shy." He waved his goons out the door, stalking out behind them.

Ace stayed frozen in place, barely breathing until the car pulled away. Then he strode out, slamming the rotting door and unlocking his Lexus.

The Lexus his boss was paying for.

He had to retrench and find that money. As he saw it, he had one last-ditch option, and it was a bold one.

The light was about to shine into the darkness and blind them all.

⌒⌒⌒

Mom had busied herself with laundry, doubtless convincing herself that there was nothing dangerous afoot. Katie sat on the couch, Sig at the ready, observing the police car out the front window. She really needed a glass of sweet tea and a sandwich, but she wasn't about to leave her watchful post.

The welcome sight of Ace's sleek grey Lexus nearly brought tears to her eyes. "He's here!" she shouted to no one in particular. After struggling to get up and get her foot moving, she made her way to the front door to meet him.

But he didn't knock. She moved to the window and caught a glimpse of his back and arm as he pulled the apartment door closed behind him. What was he doing? Maybe he was going to install the glass in the door, or maybe he was hungry.

She texted him:

Katie: *We have plenty of food over here if you want some lunch.*

She continued to stand by the window as the police unit slowly pulled away. Leaning on her good leg, she watched the apartment door for a solid ten minutes before giving up. No text. No sign of Ace.

What had happened?

After unloading and storing most of his weapons, Ace stripped to his T-shirt and threw himself onto the couch, letting his endorphin high slowly ebb away. He pictured waves on a Caribbean beach, a pastel-painted cottage he could rent with his payout from this job. Or a relaxing weekend in Connecticut in the fall, taking in the sights.

Only thing was, Katie's flaming hair and smiling face intruded into each vision.

He had to get real. There was only one way for him to get out of here alive, and that was to find the money.

Reading over Katie's text, he made a decision. Uncomfortable as it was, embarrassing as it was, he had go through with it.

It was time to come clean to Esther Sue McClure.

He made minimal eye contact as he ate his late lunch of a grilled cheese sandwich and tomato soup. Katie seemed to want to talk, but what could he say? That he'd just returned from a meeting with her dad's fake-dead partner? That a crooked FBI agent had gotten him out of prison early so he'd be in his debt?

Anxiety seemed to emanate from Katie, from her nervous finger-tapping to her frequent glances out the window. Of course she was worried—she hadn't found the money for Anatoly's men. Just like he hadn't found it for Jim.

Esther Sue finished her sandwich and stood. "I need to switch my laundry over. Excuse me."

Ace stood as well, trying to ignore Katie's startled look. "Mrs. McClure, would you mind if we talked some about my payment and things?" It was partly true.

Esther Sue ran a hand through her light hair. "Of course, dear. Let's talk in the office, shall we?"

He felt bad about leaving Katie in the dust, but she didn't need to know the truth. Yet.

Mrs. McClure shut the office door tightly, then sat in her husband's leather chair. She crossed her hands, fixing him with an inquisitive stare. "Now, how about you tell me what's really going on?"

He was taken aback. "What do you mean?"

She gave a half-smile. "I grew up with three brothers, honey. I know when a man's trying to hide something."

A picture flashed through his mind—that of Mrs. McClure sitting at the fire-pit with her husband and Jim Chrisman. Would she have known if Sean was lying to her? What about Jim? He had to ask.

"Mrs. McClure, I need you to tell me everything you know about Jim Chrisman."

Her pale blue eyes widened. "Good gracious. Well, not to

speak ill of the dead, but he always seemed too good to be true—slick, you know. Though maybe that made him a good FBI agent. But his jokes always seemed to have an edge—a sharp, pointed edge. I remember he really burned my biscuits the one time he decided to be sarcastic about the way Katie walked. I'm afraid I lost my temper and told him if he didn't apologize, he'd never set foot in my house again. He said he was sorry, but it left a bad taste in my mouth that a grown man could be that cruel."

Ace nodded. Everything that man did left a bad taste in his mouth. Shifting forward, he said, "I need to be honest with you."

She rested her arms on the desk. "Please do. I'm listening."

How many times had Granny said that same phrase to him? How many times had he unburdened his soul to her like she was some kind of priest? Here he was, back in the same position, seeking absolution.

"Mrs. McClure, I came here with less than honest intentions. I'm not a trained bodyguard, but I can handle firearms and I'm fairly popular with ladies. I was instructed to infiltrate your home and search for money that was concealed here before your husband's death. Dirty money, hidden by none other than your husband's partner, Jim Chrisman."

She sucked in her breath, but didn't speak. He continued.

"It's not something I chose to do, believe me. It's something I had to do to keep my freedom. I won't elaborate on my situation, but suffice it to say, someone powerful holds the strings to my future." He thumped his fist on the desk, dark anger brewing as he remembered Jim's smug look. "Brace yourself, Mrs. McClure. That someone is Jim Chrisman. Sean was right to want to look into his death, but maybe not for the reasons you thought. It wasn't a murder, but a faked death."

She fell back in the chair, one hand flying to her chest. "No. Does that mean…?"

He answered her unasked question. "I don't know if someone killed Sean. Jim has never admitted as much. But the thing is, he's after the money, along with the mob boss who stole it in a bank heist."

"How much money are you talking about?"

"1.5 million dollars."

She vehemently shook her head. "No. There is no way Sean had that money. Our bank account was depleted paying for his funeral expense. I've been living on his life insurance, but I have to get a job soon. I haven't told the kids yet."

He stood, pacing the room. "Jim said he hid it on the *Vixen*. He's convinced it's there, but I've checked."

"So that's what you were doing on the boat." She drew a deep breath. "You've been using my daughter, haven't you?" Her eyes swam with sudden tears.

He bowed his head. "Yes. I have."

She gasped, noisily yanking three tissues from the nearby box before bursting into a rainstorm of tears. "I…thought—I thought you were good for her."

He wished the floor would open and swallow him up. "I honestly hope I can be. I've realized I care more for Katie's safety than for my own. I want to get Jim and the mobsters away from your family. That's why I had to ask you outright."

Esther Sue examined him, sniffing and blowing her nose. Finally, she nodded. "I believe you. But I can't help you. Sean told me nothing about money or that bank case. Just that he wondered about Jim's death." A fresh burst of sobs ensued.

He nodded slowly. It was decided, then. As always, he had a plan of action. Not a safe plan, but it would be worth it if the McClures were finally left alone. He would get the gears in motion tomorrow.

But today, he had a shooting date with a certain redheaded librarian.

9

Katie tried to hide her surprise as Ace emerged, remnants of a smile on his face. What had he talked to Mom about? Surely he wouldn't have asked to...no, that was ridiculous. They hadn't even had one real date yet.

"Let's go shooting," he said.

"Is that wise, do you think? Is Mom okay?"

"I hate to burst your bubble, but it seems like you're the only one those goons are stalking, my dear. And I'll be with you, so you'll have nothing to worry about."

Warmth infused her. Yes, she was safe with Ace.

"Okay, let's get going. I'll tell Mom goodbye."

"No need. She went back to her room and I told her where we're headed. She said to be careful."

"That's my momma." She packed up the Sig. "After you, my knight in shining armor."

After two hours shooting at the range, Ace was convinced Katie had underestimated her skills. It was very possible her aim was even better than his. She had shot all his guns, even the larger .45, and had managed to keep them steady—barely a kick. This West Virginia girl could certainly hold her own in a firefight.

As they slid into the Lexus, he gave in to an idea that had been kicking around for days. "What do you say we go out to eat—on me? Anyplace good around Hemlock Creek?"

Her green eyes danced. "Sure, over in Lewisburg there are quite a few places. Are you looking to get all gussied up or just go somewhere casual?"

He smiled, briefly covering her hand with his. "Actually, I was hoping we could both get dressed up. I've seen Molly looking glitzy, but not you. I have a feeling you'd outshine her."

Her hand drew back a bit. Unlike most of the women he'd known, Katie didn't wear her feelings on her sleeve. He couldn't read her easily. She seemed to like him, but what if she was being all Southern-friendly, simply tolerating his presence until he left?

Tolerating him—like his parents had. The thought crushed him.

He shifted into gear and tried to focus on the winding roads. Glancing in his rearview, he noticed a blue SUV that was zooming up too close to his bumper. Did all these locals drive like demons?

Long fingers wrapped around his hand where it rested on the gear shift, distracting him, pulling him back. "Thanks for taking me shooting. I needed the reminder I'm not helpless. And yes, I know just the restaurant we can go to."

Her honeyed voice, soft with light Southern accents, melted something inside him. He sensed the kind of unconditional acceptance he'd only known with Granny.

As he turned to meet her eyes, the SUV rammed straight into his bumper, sending the Lexus skidding... directly toward a 400-foot drop off the side of the mountain.

⸙

Katie could only think to scream one word: "Right!"

He jerked the wheel that direction. The car flipped around into the other lane, pinning his door against the solid rock on the inside of the mountain.

The SUV sped around them as she tried to control her frantic breathing. This was no accident. After a moment's silence, she managed to croak out a few words.

"Such a close call. I'm so sorry."

He shot her a dark look. "*Do not* say sorry. It's not your fault. I should've suspected they were up to no good, driving so close."

Grasping the wheel, he lightly pushed on the gas. When the car revved, he maneuvered it out of the ditch and into its respective lane. He drove a couple minutes before finding a pull-off area, where he turned the car back toward home.

"Thank the Lord no one else was coming," she said.

He stared straight ahead. "The Lord had nothing to do with this."

She shook her head. "Yes, He did. He protected us."

"You're so sure, aren't you?" His voice held no reprimand, just incredulity.

Hesitating, she responded honestly. "Not always. Sometimes I wonder why He lets those horrible things happen. But I'm starting to believe it's always for a bigger plan…kind of a greater good."

He nodded, dark bangs falling in his eyes. "Granny felt that way too. And to tell the truth, I kind of believe it myself. It's the only way to make sense of the stuff that happens. But then another part of me wants to rail against a God who would do that."

"He's not the bad guy," she said.

Silence blanketed the car. It was like she'd struck a nerve, but why?

Their near-fatal wreck had only crunched the bumper, but as a side effect, it steamrolled any illusions Ace had been operating under.

Anatoly's men would not give up. And they weren't going to be patient.

Daydreams he'd had about a leisurely dinner with a fancied-up Katie were quickly replaced with battle plans.

He would take the fight to the oppressors. He would end this thing. And in the process, he would wound and possibly even break the one person he now cared for the most—the person he might even love.

He prayed God would forgive him for what he was about to do to Katie McClure.

As the doorbell rang, Mom went to answer it, leaving Katie alone with Molly as she prepared for her date.

Molly secured her sister's low, patent-leather heel. "This too tight?"

She shook her head, glancing at the mirror to take in her curled hair, her jewel-green sheath dress, and the sparkling diamond bracelet Molly had lent her. A trifle from a rich suitor, no doubt.

Molly smiled. "Don't be so nervous. You look choked with fear. You should date more often, stay in the swing of things."

Katie gave a short laugh, unwilling to explain she was still shell-shocked from a near-fatal crash. Molly would only freak out and report back to Mom. She tried to act glib. "No, thanks. Have you seen the guys who tend to ask me out?"

"Good point." Molly stood. "So what's up with Brandon?"

"What do you mean? I just talked to him the other day—he's keeping busy with work."

Molly hesitated. "Oh, nothing."

Katie gave her sister a look. "What are you—"

Mom knocked lightly at the bedroom door. "There's a handsome young man here to see you, Katie Beth. Best not keep him waiting."

Nodding, Katie glowered again at Molly and stalked toward the door. The heels threw her off balance and made her limp a bit more, but at least they fit comfortably.

Ace stood just inside the front door, practically hidden behind a huge bouquet of sunflowers.

She beamed. "My favorite! How did you know?"

"Just a guess. Seemed to fit you," he murmured.

Molly, close on her heels, exclaimed, "I've never seen anything so beautiful! Great taste, Ace." She took the flowers when Katie handed them over to her, blowing a kiss to both. "Have fun, you two."

Mom emerged with her camera. "Wait—hold those flowers, Katie. You two stand together."

Feeling like she was heading to the prom, Katie did as requested, trying not to burst into laughter at Ace's whispered instructions. "Give me a librarian pose," he said. "Pretend the flowers are a box of books. Now, smile, you top model, you."

When they finally took their leave, she was glad darkness had fallen so she couldn't see the damage to the rental car. One more reminder of their target status.

He opened the door. "You look amazing. Wait—that's a boring word. You look...striking. Staggering. Stupendous. And other 's' words."

She laughed, sinking into the seat. "I hope only good ones. You're on a real roll tonight."

"I plan to make you laugh loud and often, Katie McClure. Let's pretend like we're not in danger and enjoy ourselves. Although rest assured, I'm packing heat." He shut her door and strode around, settling into the driver's seat.

His fitted navy suit and light blue tie made him look like a millionaire. She held her breath as he turned on the interior light and leaned toward her, so close his breath brushed her cheek. He spoke quietly. "Just know that no matter what happens, nothing will change the way I feel about you."

Those incredible lips moved closer and he pressed a soft, open kiss on her cheek. If she turned her head, her lips would meet his…

He abruptly flipped off the light and started the car.

The man was completely unreadable. How could she ever fall for someone so mysterious?

And yet she already had.

❧❧❧

Digging into the crab dip appetizer with her slice of garlic bread, Katie seemed unaware of the thrall she held over him. When a stray breadcrumb stuck to her lip, he automatically reached up and brushed it off with his thumb.

"Um…I think I got some of your lipstick," he said, trying not to focus on those red lips.

Blotting at her mouth with a napkin, she sighed. "Molly tried to fix me up with long-wearing lipstick but it's useless, given how I like to eat." She gave him that mega-watt smile.

He wanted to touch those nearly-naked lips again, slower. He wanted to embrace her for the woman she was—the woman with the hopeful spirit and wide-open heart. He wanted to kiss her all over that beautiful face, to crush her lean body into his, taking away all her fear.

Instead, he took a long gulp of water, which promptly went down the wrong pipe.

As his hacking intensified, she walked over to pound him on the back. "Do I need to do the Heimlich? I took First Aid in high school."

"I'm...not...choking," he said between coughs. "Just...wrong pipe."

Taking a couple more sips of water, he finally regained a modicum of control. He gave a forced smile to the handful of customers and to their waiter, who stood at the ready.

Katie returned to her seat, grinning.

"Am I really that distracting?" she joked.

Yes. Yes, she was.

⚬⚭⚮⚭⚬

When their steak arrived, Katie turned the conversation back to Ace. "So tell me all about New York City. And please chew each bite carefully so we don't have a repeat of your earlier episode."

He laughed, then went on to describe the soaring buildings near his postage-stamp apartment, the running trails he took in the park, and his favorite modern art gallery. As he spoke, she was swept up in a vision of the life she'd always wanted. Big-city. Big danger. Fighting crime at the highest level.

Was that what Dad had wanted, too? Maybe that explained why he had traveled so much. Or why he would have been tempted to steal that money. Her mind wandered as he continued to speak.

"...but the street vendor on my corner sells the most amazing gyros," he said. "Plenty of meat and thick pita...Katie? Something wrong?"

"What? No. That is, I was just thinking of how I'm not the only one who turned out like my dad. Brandon loves new adventures and traveling places, too."

His eyes pulled hers in. "I would love to take you to see Manhattan."

She laughed it off. "I'd just be deadweight. I would probably fall onto the subway tracks as I tried to board."

"No, you wouldn't. Stop being so hard on yourself. How about this—I promise I'll take you to New York City someday."

She could tell he was in earnest, but what did that mean for them? Was he proposing a long-term relationship? Why didn't he come out with it frankly, the way he said everything else?

"What are you saying?"

He held her gaze. "I'm saying I want to travel with you. I want to give you adventures outside West Virginia."

Now she mirrored his seriousness. "Sorry, but I don't travel with men, unless they're related to me."

He spoke so softly, she barely caught it. "Or if you're married to them."

"Yes." She leaned across the empty bread plate. "Unless I'm married to them."

10

A strange car was parked outside and the house was aglow with lights when they returned. Though Ace was anxious to see if anything had happened, he needed to take care of something first. Something personal.

"Wonder what's up?" Katie reached for the door handle.

He stretched out a hand, clasping her arm. Chill bumps covered it.

"Are you cold?" he asked.

"No, not really." She raised her eyes to his. They were barely visible in the reflected light from the porch.

Hypnotized, he ran his hand up to her head, gently tugging her face closer. Time seemed to slow as he traced her lips, then lowered his mouth to hers.

She didn't respond. Had he misread her?

But then her hand gripped his sleeve. The pressure from her lips grew stronger, insistent. Confident and womanly.

He was swept into a world where everything seemed to make sense, to fit together. There was nothing to do but respond to the force that could both master him and repair him. Tears actually filled his eyes.

A sharp rapping on the window put an abrupt halt to their enchantment. Straightening up, he wiped off the foggy glass and cracked the window.

A skinny, bearded redhead stood there, giving him a murderous glare. "Let me guess—you're the Yankee bodyguard."

"No way." Katie leaned over. "Brandon?"

⁂

As Mom served an impromptu tray of cheese, crackers, and grapes, Brandon explained his unexpected appearance.

"After I talked to you, I started thinking about things, sis. If those mobsters wanted money, and if Dad didn't take it, that meant they wouldn't give up. So I did the one thing I knew you hadn't—I contacted the FBI and told them everything."

Ace dropped heavily onto the couch. Katie followed suit, taking off her heels.

"They'll be here in the morning. I'll meet with them and figure out a plan to find these Russian gangsters." Brandon hitched up his cargo-style jeans. "Hey, Mom, I could really use some Dr. Pepper."

Mom smiled, ruffling Brandon's overgrown hair. "It's in the pantry. I always keep some, just in case."

As Mom locked an arm in Brandon's and headed for the kitchen, Katie focused on the silent man by her side. From the sour look on his face, she figured he was really upset by their interruption in the car. She hadn't wanted the kiss to end, either, but where would it have led?

Why did she have to be attracted to someone who was such a mess spiritually? He said he'd believed in Jesus at a young age, but his growth had been stunted when his godly grandma died. Was God using their time together to point Ace back to Him? If so, she wasn't the best person to guide him.

Her brother's deep voice filled the kitchen. Brandon was someone else who was messed up and disillusioned by life. And yet he'd contacted the FBI, probably because he didn't believe Dad had taken that money. Kind of ironic she had switched perspectives with her brother on this one. Usually he had nothing good to say about Dad's work, and she had to be the one defending it.

Ace nudged her elbow with his. "Sorry. I was a little lost in thought. But that was...unforgettable...out there in the car." His eyes were a quiet blue blaze, focused on hers.

She felt like hugging him, hard. She wanted to kiss the joy back into his life. She needed to tuck her hand into his safe, strong grip.

"Tomorrow is the day," he murmured.

"What day?"

"The day you have to contact Anatoly's men with news. I copied the note before I gave it to the police. By the way, I plan to call in another police unit for you tomorrow."

"Why? Won't you be here?"

Brandon sauntered back in, carrying a huge bowl of homemade popcorn. "Look what I talked Mom into making for me. You gotta try this, Ace." He extended the bowl.

As the men fell into an easy conversation about whitewater rafting, she zoned out, focusing on the words Ace hadn't said. The words that would rip her apart when they were finally spoken aloud.

He was leaving.

Thanks to his reckless consumption of Dr. Pepper, Ace spent his final night in the garage apartment pacing and worrying. He knew what he had to do, but the logistics of his plan were tricky. How could he ever explain things to Katie?

He had replayed their kiss so many times. Her reticence had morphed into a certainty that staggered him. He wasn't worthy of such a gift—such unfettered approval. She didn't know the truth. And yet he wanted another kiss, another chance to prove he was the man she thought he was.

He finally crashed on the couch, but his alarm went off at five. Peering out the window, he saw a car and a black van out front.

The Feds were here.

Katie cut into her boiled eggs, meticulously removing the yolks she didn't care for. "You want these?"

Ace shook his head, but Brandon charged into the kitchen and swiped them. "My fave."

"Did you see that the FBI's here?" she asked.

Brandon nodded, popping a coffee pod into the coffeemaker. "Heading out after I eat. You two hanging around today?"

She crunched into a crisp piece of bacon. "I thought we could check the *Vixen* one more time. What do you think, Ace?"

When he turned to her, she stopped chewing. Her mind and her mouth froze when she registered the remorseful look on his face.

"I can't stay. I have to fly back today. Work."

That was *it*? That was all the explanation, all the farewell she got? How could he casually throw their relationship away? Because it was more than a friendship—his kiss last night had made that clear.

Mom padded in, wearing her favorite moccasin slippers. She took in her daughter's face. "What's going on?"

Katie could barely articulate the words. "Ace is leaving today."

Mom teared up, placing a hand on Ace's shoulder. "Oh, honey, we are going to miss you around here. Won't be the same without you."

Brandon chimed in. "Yeah, dude, I know we just met and all, but I feel like I know you. Which is more than I thought I'd be able to say about a New Yorker. Oh—I hope you enjoy those baseball cards. To tell the truth, I didn't even really look at them when Dad gave them to me. Just not my thing."

Seeing her family rally around Ace made it even harder. They all liked him. He wasn't some outsider, coming in and looking down on their way of life. He was like one of them.

Her words came out plaintively, like a whimper. "But Molly won't even get to say goodbye." Why did that suddenly bother her?

He took her hand, setting her emotions roiling. "I'll be in touch, I promise. Maybe I can come down during my Christmas vacation? It's not like I'll have any family events going on."

She couldn't choke out a response.

Mom hugged him. "Of course. You're always welcome here, Ace." She gave him a cryptic look Katie didn't understand.

Had their kiss meant nothing at all to him? He was just going to say goodbye and walk out of her life?

Brandon shoved his fourth piece of bacon in his mouth, then stopped cold, taking a long look at her. "Sis, you okay?"

She stood, unable to comprehend why someone she had grown so close to could abandon her like this. That wasn't love. That wasn't even like.

She fumbled down the hall toward her room. Slamming the door, she let her thoughts scream even louder. What did it matter if Anatoly's men tried to blow her away? She was never leaving this one-horse town anyway.

Ace whisked around the apartment, jamming everything into his capacious suitcases and trying to shove thoughts of Katie from his mind. He had to do this…in fact, he was doing it for *her*, but she would probably never know. He couldn't stick around here.

As he loaded one gun and strapped it on, there was a knock on the door. He opened it to find Molly, looking downright dangerous in her stilettos and black leather jacket.

"Sit down," she said, shoving her way past him and nearly impaling him with a long fingernail. "We have to talk."

Crossing her legs at an angle as if she were posing for a glamour shot, Molly launched into a diatribe, complete with emphatic hand motions.

"You're a handsome guy, Ace—and you know it." She smiled at his surprise. "Takes one to know one, bub. What I have to say, before you so rudely take off and leave my pining sister in the dust, is that Katie doesn't just fall for anyone. After that foot injury, she closed up a corner of her heart. Then when Dad died, she put up a No Trespassing sign and wrapped the entire thing in police tape. No men have gotten in. Ever." She paused, scrutinizing him. "But here's the deal: she must see something in you that runs deeper than looks."

He took a couple deep, calming breaths, trying to figure out which way Molly was going with this. She didn't slow down, nearly boring holes into him with her stare.

"What I'm telling you is that if you walk away from this, it will crush her. She doesn't even know how in love she is yet, but I can tell. Sisterly intuition. And here's something else. I can tell you're a good match for her. She's happier when she's with you, and she's more...*herself*." She stood and started pacing, sharp heels clicking on the floor. "And so help me, if you leave her in the lurch, I..." She made a wringing gesture with her hands.

He couldn't stop himself. He laughed outright.

Fire blazed into her cheeks. "How *dare* you laugh about my sister?"

He held up a hand, rushing to explain before Molly's anger got the better of her. "I'm not laughing about Katie. I believe I love her too, crazy as that sounds. That's why I have to go."

She raised one eyebrow, but waited for him to explain.

11

A knock sounded on Katie's bedroom door and she cracked it.

Ace stood outside, an inscrutable look on his face. "I wanted to say goodbye before I pack my car. I did tell your sister goodbye and she's waiting in the kitchen to talk with you."

She looked at the half of his face she could see. She tried to memorize his features, while at the same time pretending not to care. "Thanks. Thanks for everything. Bye."

"I'm sorry this is so abrupt," he said. "I'm going to talk with the FBI guys for a few minutes, tell them what's happened, then I have to get rolling. They'll make sure you're protected from here on out."

She couldn't bite back her bitter words. "Washing your hands of us, are you?"

He put a hand on the door, opening it so she could see his entire face. His eyes were filled with concern and a deeper emotion, but she wouldn't be so stupid as to call it love.

"I'm not. I promise I'm not. I'll never get you out of my head, Katie McClure."

She slammed the door.

Minutes dragged into an hour as he talked with the FBI agents. Now the whole story was out. Jim's fake death. His deal with Jim to save himself from prison. His placement in the McClure home and his subsequent failure to find the bank heist money.

It was almost time for the FBI to take over, but not quite. He had one last job to do. He owed it to Katie.

She watched the van doors close as Ace climbed in. Brandon was already talking with other agents in the living room. It was quite a force they'd brought out, she'd give them that. Probably out of respect for her dad...and he was worthy of respect, since it was obvious he'd never absconded with illegal funds.

What a fool she'd been, falling for Ace. Searching for money she knew her dad didn't take. And yet...

Yet he had protected her tirelessly. He had told her things she figured he hadn't told anyone else. He'd opened up to her, hadn't he?

And if she was honest with herself, he had been the invigorating breeze that had blown many of her cobwebs of self-doubt away. She had seen God's hand of protection, remembered what it felt like to be loved for who she was.

She had to tell him that.

Propelled by the obscure emotions she was still processing, Katie pulled on her low boots, then scrawled a note for Mom and dropped it on her bed. She headed out the back door and snuck around the back of her apartment to avoid scrutiny by the FBI agents. Creeping toward the Lexus, she could see a couple bags lying on the back floor, as well as a blanket and pillow.

An idea began to simmer, then it quickly combusted into a blaze. It was perfect. This would be her greatest adventure yet. She smiled at her own boldness, her spontaneity. How very un-librarianesque of her.

She would tell him she loved him, let the chips fall where they may. Maybe he would choose to skip the flight and stay, like the ending of a romantic movie. But then again, maybe she'd have to catch a cab home from the airport.

She didn't care.

She needed closure. And probably one last kiss.

Mrs. McClure stood on the porch, waving as Ace thudded the car door shut and buckled himself in. No sign of Katie. It was probably for the best.

Using his newly-developed mountain driving skills, he made good time, maneuvering the curvy roads like a pro. Glancing at the canopy of green trees arching near the side of the road, his stomach clenched. Such a wild elegance here in Hemlock Creek. It was an unaffected natural beauty of the most powerful kind. He pictured Katie's hair, blowing in the wind. Her eyes, sparkling with amusement and candor. She embodied that unaffected beauty that brought out his most protective feelings.

If only he had more to offer her. If only his life hadn't been derailed by an unwarranted prison sentence. He could have been an upstanding citizen with nothing blotting his record.

Now he had more than a blot, he had made a deal with the devil. At least it would soon be over.

The car slowed. Had they already arrived at the Lewisburg airport? Katie didn't dare raise up from under the blanket until Ace had gotten out. She didn't want to alarm a man who always carried a gun.

Even with the air-conditioning on, the wool blanket she'd hid under felt stifling. Though it carried the comforting smell of its owner, she had to get out from under it. When the car door slammed, she barely shifted, breathing in his scent one more time before exposing her mouth and one eye.

This was probably a dumb idea. She might very well scare him out of his mind, since he'd been in hyper-vigilant bodyguard mode for so long. She wouldn't pop out and open the door...she'd just ease out.

The trunk slammed and she heard him walking away. No! She'd waited too long!

She struggled to sit up, stiffening in fear as she peeped out at the view.

This wasn't the airport. Vines tangled around a large, dilapidated building that was surrounded by trees. One large maple tree was actually growing out of the roof.

A black car was parked off to the side of the building, and Ace was heading straight for it, pulling his rolling suitcase behind him.

Had he found the money and contacted Anatoly's men? Was this some kind of drop?

Had he betrayed them all?

Barely rising above the window ledge, she held her breath, watching two larger men exit the black car. They were holding Uzis, but they didn't look like the same men from the library.

A man emerged from the front seat, smiling like the Cheshire Cat. Sandy blond hair, deep tan, ridiculous Hawaiian shirt.

She'd know him anywhere. Jim Chrisman. She gagged, nearly losing her breakfast. So Dad's partner hadn't had cancer, and he wasn't murdered, as Dad had suspected. In fact, he'd never died in the first place. And Ace must have known all along.

A dark blue SUV raced up from the far side of the parking lot, screeching to halt in front of Ace and the others. Three armed men jumped out, also toting heavier artillery. They formed a loose circle around the initial collaborators.

As Ace stared at the newcomers, she couldn't miss the look of panic in his eyes. When he slowly raised his hands in the air, she dropped to the floor, pulled the blanket over herself, and started praying furiously. She had no weapons, and Ace had no chance.

He had never been so nervous, even though he was the one who'd secretly invited Anatoly to this rendezvous. He carried only one pistol and they could mow him down faster than he could blink, despite the bulletproof vest the Feds had loaned him.

The FBI lurked somewhere, listening to this exchange through his earpiece. They knew his suitcase was stuffed with empty Dr. Pepper bottles, so the moment he opened it, he'd be toast if they didn't get to him first.

But he was banking on one thing: Anatoly wasn't the kind to cut a deal. Jim might try to wheedle his way out of this, but the Russian would find it glaringly apparent who had orchestrated the theft of his bank money.

Anatoly scooted out of his seat, his corpulent stomach spilling over his belt. He carried a smaller gun but had no need of it, given his well-armed henchmen.

He took a wide stance and shouted. "Jim Chrisman! You are a—" Harshly punctuated Russian words spewed forth. Anatoly's men understood them and snickered.

Ace stood between the powerful men, not budging. Let the titans clash this one out.

Jim gave his ingratiating smile. "Anatoly. Let's work something out, like men."

The large Russian cackled. "You are no man. You are a coward who hid behind his partner. So scared you had to play dead." He took a step closer. "Today I will show you what you had to fear."

Jim held up his hands. "Now hold up, big fella. Let's see what my stooge has brought me. Oh wait, I haven't made introductions." He pointed. "Ace, this is Anatoly. Anatoly, this is the clueless sap I landed in jail, then pulled out of there so he could find my money. A real ladies' man."

Blood rushed into Ace's ears, making his head pound. He had been such a fool. The invisible lowlife who had framed him years ago was the exact same man who had released him. Jim Chrisman had no intention of letting him go, even if he did have the money. He would send him right back to prison.

If only Anatoly would take the first shot.

Closing his eyes, he prayed silently. Peace washed over him and he knew he still shared Katie's faith in a loving God—a Father who watched out for His children. He promised to go back to Katie and make things right if he survived this encounter. But if not, she would eventually know what he had done to protect her family.

Jim repeated himself, obviously antsy. "I said it's time to show us the money, Ace. You do it or my men will do it for you."

Ace wheeled his piece of luggage closer, leaning down as if he would unzip it. Taking a deep breath, he gripped the sides, hurling the suitcase to the ground directly in front of Anatoly.

Anatoly jolted back but quickly recovered his composure as he realized Ace had given him the loot. He smiled like a doting parent. "You did well, my boy." He spoke one Russian word and reached for the suitcase.

As he did so, a single shot rang out. Ace dropped to the ground, a burning sensation spreading across his head. Pain blinded him. He rolled in the general direction of the SUV, hoping to slide under the oversized vehicle as a volley of shots unleashed.

Something warm and sticky dribbled into his eyes. He swiped at it, then realized it was blood.

He'd been shot in the head.

As the world grew fuzzy, he took comfort in one thing: Katie was safe.

12

"Oh, Lord, please no. Please don't take him, Lord." Katie squeezed Ace's limp hand in hers, staring at the blood still spackling his hastily-cleaned face.

Two FBI medics spoke rapidly to one another. She could only catch blips of the conversation.

"Another unit of blood."

"That's right."

"Is he responsive?"

Ace's hand shifted slightly under hers. "He's alive!" she shouted.

The dark-haired medic smiled her way. "Yes, he is. He got lucky. That bullet only grazed his head and ear. It'll take a little stitching, but he'll survive. He was exceptionally brave, going up against two powerful criminals."

She hugged Ace's hand to her face, kissing it. "Yes, he is. The most devoted bodyguard ever."

When Ace opened his eyes, a bearded man with wild red hair was peering at his face. Where was he?

But the moment Brandon spoke, he recognized him.

"Dude! You're awake!"

Lowering his gaze from the faded hospital ceiling, Ace smiled as the three McClure women rushed his way.

"Thank the Lord!" Mrs. McClure said.

"You scoundrel." Molly winked. "I knew if anyone could pull it off, you could."

Katie leaned over and brushed his forehead with a kiss. "When you're all better, you're going to explain why you told my sister about your meeting of imminent doom, but not me. And then I'll tell you about this really *interesting* car ride I had…"

Much as he struggled to stay alert, his eyes fluttered closed. "Love…you," he mumbled.

Suddenly, Katie's strong voice was right next to his ear. "I love you too," she said.

<hr/>

Two days later, Katie explained the events of that day to Ace one more time, even as she lightly traced his stitches. They were healing fast.

"From what the agents said, Jim shot at Anatoly and the bullet grazed you. It killed Anatoly on the spot. Then you dropped and the men blasted into a shooting free-for-all, which came to an abrupt halt when the FBI agents showed up. Jim didn't get hit, because he hid in the car—the loser. Now he's heading straight for prison." Her voice dropped. "He still swears he had nothing to do with Dad's death."

He gripped her hand and she felt renewed encouragement.

She edged closer to his leg from her perch on the side of the couch. "They investigated your record and said it's officially expunged. It was obvious Jim set you up so he could get to us."

He adjusted his legs to make more room for her, then took a slow sip of unsweetened iced tea, thankful he was around to enjoy it. "But I don't understand what happened to that 1.5 million. Jim swears he hid it on your dad's boat."

"I know, it's so weird. There's no way Dad could've spent all that. Mom would have known. And by the way, Mom came clean and said you'd told her about Jim before your clandestine meeting with him. Did everyone know but me?"

Catching the last of their conversation, Brandon strode over, dropping his overstuffed rucksack to the floor. "I knew nothing, sis—promise. I just wanted to get the FBI in on things. Little did I know your bodyguard would suggest another plan to them." He gave Ace a high-five before his look turned serious. "You're a real hero, man. I have mad respect for you. I hate to fly out now, but I need to get back. Hey—maybe I'll see you around sometime? I'm thinking I might come back in October. To tell the truth, I miss fall in these mountains."

Katie beamed, thankful that her brother seemed to be feeling more connected to his family. "I hope you do. We don't see you enough."

Brandon shoved his aviator sunglasses on. "I was pretty wrong about Dad. I mean, he probably only wanted me to play baseball so we could do something together. And I pushed him away. Meanwhile, there he was, serving with an utterly corrupt partner who wound up ripping off a mob boss and staging his own death."

Ace reached for the coffee table, retrieving the bag of baseball cards. "That reminds me. I haven't even looked over these yet, but you should keep them. They were never meant for me."

Brandon hesitated, then silently nodded. As he took the partially-opened bag, the contents spilled out on the floor.

Katie bent over to shuffle the cards back into a pile. One caught her eye. "Hey—how cool is this? This card says it's from 1951."

"Could I see that?" Ace asked. He examined it as she began to sort cards by year.

"There are several with the older dates," she said.

Brandon took off his sunglasses, plopping down on the floor nearby. "You're right, sis."

Ace looked incredulous, barely holding the card between thumb and forefinger as if it were on fire. "This one is a Joe Jackson card of the Chicago White Sox."

She nodded politely, handing him another old one.

"And this is a Willie Mays," he said.

Shooting his sister a blank look, Brandon spoke up. "We really have no idea who they are, man. So you ought to keep these. They'll mean more to someone who appreciates baseball."

Ace propped himself up and grabbed at the pile of old cards.

As he shuffled through, mumbling names, Katie shrugged. She began packing the rest away in the bag.

Finally, he beamed. "Brandon, Katie—your dad was no fool. He knew about Jim and he knew about the heist money."

"What makes you say that?" She was bewildered.

He dropped the pile of cards in her lap. "Because he took it and he bought baseball cards. *Extremely valuable* baseball cards. It probably took months to get hold of all these. Just one of these could be worth up to a hundred thousand dollars or more. To avoid suspicion, he mixed them with modern cards, then packed away the bag in the attic. No one would even think to look for cards instead of cash."

Brandon sighed. "So, Dad was crooked after all?"

"No. He was smart. He was aware if the cash was found on his boat, he'd be an instant suspect in the theft. He'd look like a crooked FBI agent, and he could lose his job or even get sent to jail. So he pretended to be oblivious to Jim, meanwhile disguising the money for later."

"Still doesn't seem legit," Brandon muttered.

"I think he was probably worried about us," Katie said. "If he lost his job because of suspected theft, I'm sure the FBI would have made it hard for him to get hired anywhere."

Brandon laughed. "Come to think of it, I think he'd finally be proud of me. Suddenly I find myself very interested in baseball."

She lightly punched his arm, shaking her head. "You aren't keeping these now, bro. We have to hand them over to the FBI so they can close this case." She looked to Ace for affirmation.

He nodded, touching his stitches as if they still pained him. "It's the right thing to do. But first we should probably let your mom know."

"And Molly—she'll want to be in the loop."

He grinned. "That's for sure."

<hr />

One week later, when Ace's head was finally starting to feel normal, the FBI pulled up to the McClures' home.

The agents spontaneously broke into a round of applause as he walked out to meet them, carrying the bag of baseball cards. Katie squeezed his arm. He had never felt so respected in all his life.

The lead agent stepped up and shook his hand. "We can't tell you how much we appreciate your bravery, not to mention your discovery of the cards. Otherwise that money would've been lost forever. As a reward, the bank has agreed to let you keep your choice of two cards."

He gasped, then paused to think. "Let's see, I'll pick one for Brandon first. How about the Joe Jackson—the first card that tipped me off to what happened?"

Katie grinned. "Thanks for thinking of him."

As for himself, he knew just the one he wanted. Digging around in the bag, he found it and handed it to Katie.

"Joe DiMaggio. He didn't agree with his dad concerning his career, and he married a beautiful woman that was out of his league. I can relate."

She frowned. "What are you saying? Did you fail to tell me that you're married?"

Wrapping an arm around her slim waist, he kissed her cheek. "No, but I'll get married someday. And I have this particularly beautiful redhead in mind."

<hr />

As Ace drove off in the somewhat-battered Lexus, Molly whistled. "Good gracious, I hate to see that boy go. He was really good for you, sis."

"I know." Katie tried to hide a smile. "He's not gone forever, you know."

Molly bumped hips with her. "I hope he comes to visit. And Mom told me he's going to the police academy? I guess he's racked up some experience fighting bad guys. We all knew he was great with weapons."

"That's for sure. And strangely enough, he wants to work for a small police station—just like the one here in Hemlock Creek."

Molly quirked an eyebrow. "Wait—you mean you're not following him up to New York City? I thought you were going to bust outta this town the first chance you got."

Relishing her new zeal for life, Katie shook her head. "The dreams I was chasing weren't the right dreams for me in the first place. It hit me when I was crouching in Ace's car, praying and fearing for our lives. I'm not meant to be on the front lines like that—like Dad was."

Molly's smile widened. "I think we always knew that was the case. But we couldn't convince you of that. You just had to find yourself."

"I have—the self God made me to be. When I'm honest, I have to admit I enjoy being a librarian, I love our small town, and I like living near family. Reba will want to retire someday, and I'm already thinking of ways to modernize the library. I feel like I finally have a mission."

Molly winked. "And does that mission include a certain Ace Calhoun?"

"He just took out a Hemlock Creek library card, so I expect him to be a regular patron."

"Stop hedging! Are you two an item or what?" Molly crossed her arms, feigning anger.

Katie thought of Ace's goodbye kiss. He hadn't spoken a word, but had pulled her into his arms and gazed at her until, as if magnetized, she tipped her lips to meet his. "My future is with you," he'd murmured. "You're my hero, Katie McClure."

"And you're my champion—my ace," she'd said.

And now she was ready to face the future, unafraid. To stand tall on the feet God gave her, tipsy as those feet might be. Ace would be there to support her.

"We're more than an item." She hugged her sister. "We're engaged."

About the Author

HEATHER DAY GILBERT writes novels that capture life in all its messy, bittersweet, hope-filled glory. Born and raised in the West Virginia mountains, generational story-telling runs in her blood. Heather is a graduate of Bob Jones University and is married to her college sweetheart. Having recently returned to her roots, she and her husband are raising their three children in the same home in which Heather grew up.

Heather's Viking historical novel, *God's Daughter*, is an Amazon Norse bestseller. She is also the author of *Miranda Warning* and *Trial by Twelve*, Books One and Two in the bestselling *A Murder in the Mountains* mystery series. She has also written the *Indie Publishing Handbook: Four Key Elements for the Self-Publisher*.

You can find Heather online here:

Website:

http://heatherdaygilbert.com

Facebook Author Page:

https://www.facebook.com/heatherdaygilbert

Twitter:

@heatherdgilbert

Pinterest:

https://www.pinterest.com/heatherdgilbert/

Goodreads:

www.goodreads.com/author/show/7232683.Heather_Day_Gilbert

E-Mail:

heatherdaygilbert@gmail.com

If you enjoyed Out of Circulation, *please leave a review on your online book retailer of choice or on Goodreads at https://www.goodreads.com/book/show/28676255. Positive reviews encourage authors more than you know!*

If you're interested in who Heather pictured for Katie McClure and Ace Calhoun, check out her Pinterest board at https://www.pinterest.com/heatherdgilbert/out-of-circulation/

And for updates on the release of Undercut *and* Deadlocked, Books 2-3 *in the* Hemlock Creek Suspense *series, please sign up for Heather's newsletter at http://eepurl.com/Q6w6X*

Made in the USA
San Bernardino, CA
05 March 2017